Carolers and Corpses

Rachel Lynne

Seven Oaks Press

Copyright © 2022 by Rachel Lynne

All rights reserved.

No portion of this book may be reproduced in any form without written permission from the publisher or author, except as permitted by U.S. copyright law.

Holly Daye

A retired deputy sheriff turned events decorator; she's never met a mystery she didn't like.

The Colonel

A brindle English bulldog. He provides emotional support for Holly, has been known to dig up a clue or three, and sometimes saves the day!

Dewey Barker

Holly Daye's younger brother. A nice guy that just needs to find a good woman to keep him on the straight and narrow; or so his mama insists.

Euphemia Barker

Holly Daye and Dewey Barker's doting mama. Ms. Effie is the queen of her front porch and knows everything that happens in Sanctuary Bay; if she doesn't, then it didn't happen.

Roland Dupree

Revered and feared on the legal circuit until the shocking murder of his only son tilted his world on its axis. He's embittered and single-minded in his quest for answers and will slay any dragons standing between him and justice.

Madison Ross

The apple of her father's eye, nothing has ever upset Madison's cart until a bewitching beauty on the hunt for a sugar daddy worms her way into the older man's life and shakes the family tree.

Brianna Bellamy Ross

One-hit-wonder pop idol turned Hollywood starlet; Brianna was rocketing to fame until an affair with the wrong man crash landed her dreams. Nearly broke and blackballed, a wealthy older man could finance her way back into the cosmos, but she'll have to play wicked stepmother first.

Kay Emory

Logistics specialist and doting soccer mom, Kay Emory had it all until a freak accident took everything she held dear. Haunted by ghosts of what can never be and driven by guilt, Kay won't let anything come between her and the closure she seeks.

Felicity Simms

Retired teacher, Felicity Simms prides herself on her home, lawn, and prize- winning orchids, and if anything or anyone threatens her treasures she's not afraid to mete out punishment.

Gary Walston

A charming wife, three great kids, a beautiful home and a thriving local business, Gary has it all but, a bad investment left cracks in the façade and Gary will do anything to patch them before the walls cave in.

Vincente DeMarco

Born the handsome prince of the DeMarco family, the world is his oyster, but the pearl he covets most is the one he'll never have; unless he becomes an only child …

Valentina DeMarco

Twin to her overindulged brother, Valentina is long suffering and stable until the thing she loves most is threatened. In a fight for control of her family's business, she'll sacrifice anything to emerge victorious.

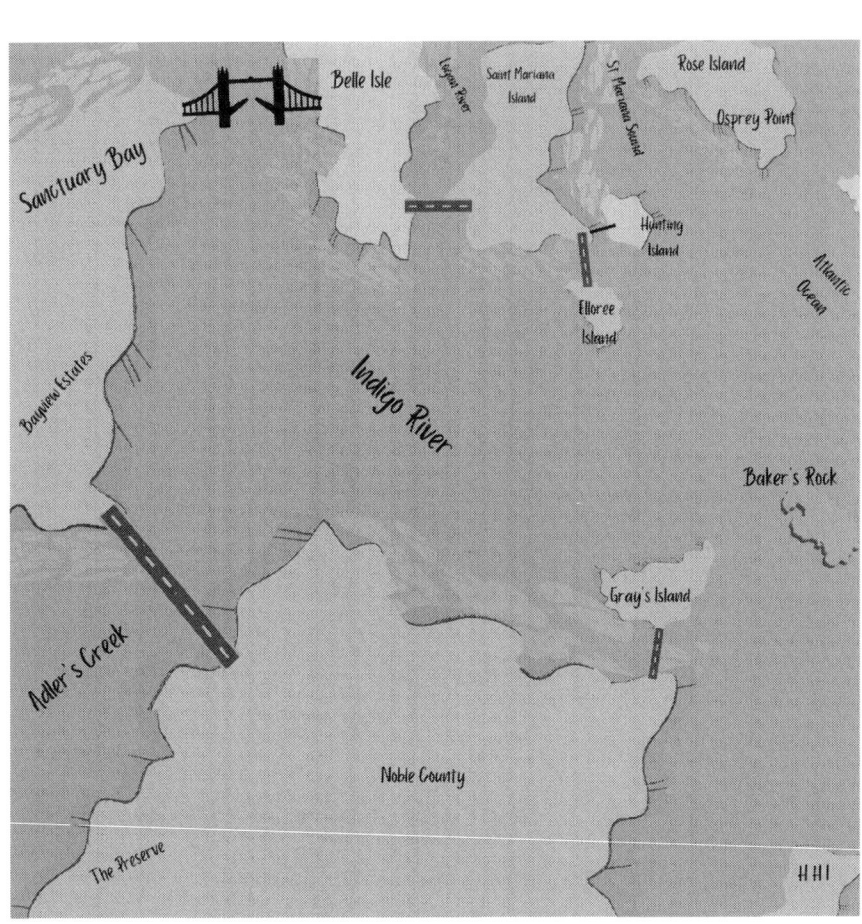

Sanctuary Bay and the Sea Islands

Sanctuary Bay Holiday Market

Contents

1. Chapter One — 1
2. Chapter Two — 13
3. Chapter Three — 31
4. Chapter Four — 46
5. Chapter Five — 57
6. Chapter Six — 67
7. Chapter Seven — 79
8. Chapter Eight — 85
9. Chapter Nine — 94
10. Chapter Ten — 111
11. Chapter Eleven — 126
12. Chapter Twelve — 140
13. Chapter Thirteen — 149
14. Chapter Fourteen — 165

15. Chapter Fifteen — 172
16. Chapter Sixteen — 180
17. Chapter Seventeen — 196
18. Chapter Eighteen — 209
19. Chapter Nineteen — 224
20. Chapter Twenty — 234
21. Chapter Twenty-One — 249
22. Chapter Twenty-two — 263
23. Chapter Twenty-three — 283
24. Chapter Twenty-four — 297

Also By — 314

Chapter One

Darkness fell over Goodwin Park as Mayor Lou Lou Tomlin climbed the steps to the stage. She waited until all the lights in the middle section of the park were extinguished before cuing the band. A hush fell over the crowd as the drumroll began. The mayor started the count, and everyone joined in. "Five, four, three, two, ..."

The opening chords of "Joy to the World" washed over us as millions of twinkling lights draped around a thirty-foot Christmas tree sprang to life and illuminated the night. Everyone cheered and started to mingle as the Noble County High School band continued to play carols.

Mama was sitting in the historical society booth with her friends and my *date* had been called to the scene of an accident, leaving my bulldog and me free to roam. Date. Was that what we'd been on before duty called Tate away? I was sure he'd thought so but, as usual, my thoughts concerning the amorous coroner for Noble County were hazy at best.

We'd been friends for years, though nothing closer than 'hey, how are ya" acquaintances until my shooting and subsequent divorce. Tate had been a godsend; supportive, knowledgeable, kind. He was still all those things, but now he also wanted to be *more than friends.*

Skirting around a rowdy group of teens, I sighed and considered my complicated relationship with the good doctor. Mama was all for it as were my best friends Connie and Jessica. My former boss and childhood friend, Craig Everette, was staying noncommittal, though when pressed he'd say that Tate was a *great guy.*

Great guy. I rolled my eyes and guided my always-hungry-for-people-food bulldog away from a food truck. I wasn't disputing the goodness of Tate Sawyer, in fact, I'd go so far as to admit I found him attractive. But, regardless of his winning ways and physical attributes, the fact remained that, less than a year ago, I had suffered a nearly fatal shooting and been left with mobility issues and PTSD.

Piling onto my problems, three months into my convalescence, my husband of thirty years decided to leave me and, adding insult to injury, the other woman was a girl two years younger than our son!

Speaking of my son. I'd run into him just before the tree lighting and he'd barely spoken three words and those were only monosyllable answers to my questions. He'd helped me find an attorney for my brother after he was accused of murdering a local podcaster while helping me decorate back in October but, aside from that, Junior had avoided me like the plague.

Discounting those handful of phone calls concerning Dewey, Junior had not willingly spoken to me since the argument we had at the family celebration for July fourth. That he'd come to Mama's at all was a testament to his love for his grandmother, but he'd been cool to me. I lost my temper and delivered a few home truths about his father.

RACHEL LYNNE

Brooks Daye had always been immature and selfish, and it was time Junior accepted it, though I should have refrained from calling his dad a filthy old pervert.

The relationship with my son had to be mended but a community event wasn't the time or place. I pushed aside my frustration over the issue and forced myself to focus on the job at hand; namely, inspecting the various activities and elements of the holiday market so that I could go home and rest.

Tents housing local organizations and charities were lined along the route leading to the far end of the park. I tried to get lost in the crowd, but Kay Emory, chairwoman of the Gray's Island Causeway Coalition, managed to spot me, or more likely The Colonel. The sad sack eyes and floppy jowls of my best buddy drew people like a magnet. I sighed and worked my way over to the booth.

"Holly!" Kay leaned over and scratched The Colonel behind the ear. "Hello you little potato." She met my gaze and smiled. "Everything looks wonderful and there's such a great turnout!"

"Thanks, Kay."

She rummaged in the bag attached to her wheelchair, pulling out a silver thermos and pouring liquid into a cup. My nose twitched as the sharp scent of mulled wine filled the air. She caught my eye and raised her glass. "Want some?"

"No thanks, smells good though." I tipped my head toward the large wooden box prominently placed on a table at the front of the tent. "How are the donations coming? Getting a good amount?"

Kay's brown eyes glowed with excitement. "People are being so generous! If they keep this up, we'll make our goal of five thousand by the end of the week!"

"That's great, Kay. It's a worthy cause, I'm sure people will continue to support it."

"I hope so, time is running out. If we don't secure our share of the funding in time, we'll lose the matching state funds and have to start the whole petitioning process again next year."

"I hope that doesn't happen." The Gray's Island Causeway had been built in the mid-1900s on unstable ground. As a result, the causeway flooded with heavy downpours and seasonal high tides, making it both a nuisance and a danger.

Kay Emory was leading the charge to get the road rebuilt. For her it was personal; traveling across the causeway during a torrential rainstorm, her car had rolled and landed in the marsh, killing her son, and leaving Kay bound to a wheelchair.

"Nor do I." A scowl darkened her face. "If only Clayton Ross hadn't died ... as chairman of the island council he was guiding the project through the proper channels, well, up until he remarried." She rolled her eyes. "God forgive me, but what was the man thinking, getting involved with *that woman*!"

I frowned. "What woman?"

"*Brianna Bellamy*, oh sorry, it's *Bellamy Ross* now."

My eyes widened at Kay's tone; she'd almost growled the woman's name. Never having met her, I knew little about Brianna Bellamy Ross except that she'd married Clayton Ross, a retired businessman and widower, a little over a year ago. He'd collapsed and died from a sudden heart attack not long after, leaving a devastated daughter and, according to the rumor mill, a merry widow.

I shook my head. "What does him marrying her have to do with his death?"

Kay rolled her eyes. "Oh, come on Holly, he was sixty-one and that woman can't be more than thirty!" Kay shook her head. "A man that age cavorting around like a young buck in heat! No wonder his heart gave out." Kay shuddered. "Poor Madison, imagine your father marrying a woman not much older than you!"

CAROLERS AND CORPSES

Since my ex-husband was dating one younger than our son I didn't have to imagine, not that I pointed that out to Kay; avoiding public speculation and gossip concerning Brooks was a point of pride with me.

I tuned back in as Kay continued to fume.

"Always prancing around in her skimpy clothes reminding people that she was a star. You know how she *really* got famous, don't you?"

My leg was starting to protest, it always did when I stood in one place too long. Even if it wasn't, my tolerance for gossip had been reached; if I ever found myself pining for the latest tidbit on the neighbors Mama could oblige.

Wanting to avoid any further discussion, I chose a white lie. "Yes, I believe so. I'm gonna have to—"

"Then you know she isn't any better than she ought to be! Why, I was talking with Valentina DeMarco yesterday and she said the Bellamy woman does yoga every morning on her dock!"

I'd backed away from the tent, hoping to make my escape, but curiosity got the better of me. I frowned at Kay. "What's wrong with doing yoga on the dock?"

Kay's eyes widened. "She does it naked!"

My mouth dropped open. "Ooooh! I bet her neighbors love that!" I bit my lip to keep from laughing. Really, naked yoga on the dock ... no wonder the ladies were all up in arms.

Kay scowled. "Felicity Simms lives next door and is fit to be tied." Kay leaned forward and lowered her voice. "She claims it's her teenaged grandson she's concerned about but it's probably that husband of hers. Give him a couple of drinks and Eugene always was a bit of a lech."

"Hmm, you might be right." I backed away. "I gotta run Kay, nice talking to you!"

"Okay, take care, Holly! Come out to the house and—"

The sound of her voice was lost in the chatter of the crowd. The Bellamy woman making waves in Gray's Island society was amusing but I had work to do and a hot tub calling my name.

Despite my aversion to gossip, I couldn't help but think about what Kay had said concerning Clayton and the Bellamy woman. As May/December romances went, it was one heck of an age gap!

Brianna was only seven years older than Ross's daughter. That he'd married the woman was brow raising, though surely water under the bridge now that he'd passed. Even though she was my

CAROLERS AND CORPSES

assistant, I'd yet to speak to Madison on the subject and hoped I wouldn't have to; it was none of my affair.

The market had a huge turnout and most of the people seemed to be heading to the same area I needed to go. The Colonel was happy to be slowed to a crawl, more time for him to sniff out dropped food, but I was chomping at the bit.

Several minutes later a break in the throng let me squeeze by the meandering visitors. I increased my pace and was about to round a corner when I heard my name called.

I turned to find Gary Walston striding toward me.

"Hey, Gary."

He smiled and patted The Colonel. "Evenin' Holly, congratulations on the market. Looks to be a huge hit."

"Thanks, everyone does seem to be enjoying themselves." I motioned behind me. "I was just checking on the decorations."

Gary nodded while digging in his pocket. "I won't keep you. Felicity Simms wanted me to ask if we can stay late tonight."

I frowned. "Stay ... you mean here at the park? What for?"

"Yeah," He paused to unwrap a piece of gum. A few seconds later a smell I associated with the holidays reached my nose. I was trying to place it when Gary started talking again. "Sorry about that." He chewed his gum a few times and then flashed a rueful smile. "Using the gum to kick the smoking habit. Anyway, our choir needs to rehearse for tomorrow's performance, and we haven't been able to get everyone together but they're all here for the tree lighting, so we thought ..."

"Ah, I see." Of all the volunteers that had helped make the holiday market a success, Gary Walston deserved a medal. I'd requested temporary poles be placed around the park so we could run market lighting. It'd been approved and the public works department had been slated to install the necessary equipment but, two days before they were to begin work, the department fell into chaos.

The ex-wife of assistant director Preston Spruill had called for a welfare check after her former spouse failed to pick up their son for a birthday celebration. From what little had been reported, it was hard to form an opinion on what had happened to the man, but the responding officers had found remnants of dinner on the kitchen table and the television blaring. That seemed suspicious to me, though Sheriff Felton had dismissed the reporter's probing questions as fear mongering.

One of the area's largest general contractors, Gary, had offered his company's services and saved the day. One good turn deserved another. I smiled. "Of course. I'll add you guys to security's list."

I'd taken a few steps toward my next inspection stop when something occurred to me. "Gary? How long do you think you'll be?"

"Maybe an hour? We'll start a little after ten when the park closes."

"Ok, that'll work. We have a company coming in tonight to replenish the fake snow, but they start at the back of the park and work their way to the entrance."

His brow furrowed. "Oh, we don't want to get in the way. We can try to do it early tomorrow. "

"Nah, it's fine. We aren't putting the stuff in the high traffic areas." I waved my hand in dismissal. "Y'all go on and use the stage but the gates will be locked so you'll need to find security to let you out."

Gary thanked me again and I continued my mission. Smiling at acquaintances and waving at neighbors, I worked my way through the crowds and headed for the eastern end of the park. I'd do a final walk through starting at the back and work my way to the parking lot. Barring mishap or mayhem, I could complete my inspection and be soaking my aching leg in the hot tub in an hour.

Chapter Two

The hour I'd estimated for completing my inspection turned into two and counting. It seemed every section I passed contained someone looking for me to solve their problems.

The dull ache in my leg had morphed into a constant throb that left me questioning the efficacy of the physical therapy I'd been faithfully attending since the beginning of November. While there was massive improvement in my mobility, my leg was still nowhere near functioning at the levels it had before I'd been shot.

Reminders of my physical limitations only served to annoy me, and an increase in aggravation was the last thing I needed at the moment. I shoved thoughts and feelings surrounding the shooting to the back of my mind and concentrated on inspecting the bonfire area.

Goodwin Park had been divided into sections with the town Christmas tree in the middle, the bonfire and other activities at the far end, and a holiday hamlet of vendor booths located nearest the entrance.

The market ran from Sunday through the following Saturday, with several special events planned. The lighting of the tree had been the featured activity for Sunday. Monday through Friday would be concerts and Christmas carol sing-alongs, story time and photo ops with Santa, and a theatrical reading of *A Christmas Carol* accompanied by live orchestration courtesy of the Noble County Chamber Ensemble.

To turn the temperate region of Sanctuary Bay, South Carolina into a winter wonderland, I'd hired a company that specialized in movie special effects. Each night after the market closed, workers would replenish a special polymer-based snow

CAROLERS AND CORPSES

by spraying a light dusting over the shrubs and trees, but I'd also brought in a machine that produced real snow.

Frosty's Kingdom was a fenced off area located in the Reindeer Games section of the market. All week long, kids who might never have seen snow could frolic in the wet stuff, and Friday night would see the families of Sanctuary Bay pitted against one another in a snowman building contest.

Along with the snow machine, I'd rented an ice-skating rink, bouncy castle, and children's train. Judging by the lines The Colonel and I walked past on our way to the bonfire; Reindeer Games was the most popular attraction.

At the farthest end of the park, I'd assembled a fire pit and on the final evening, a roaring bonfire would light the night. Pastor Duke Mobley and his biker congregation would have a booth selling smores kits and hotdogs on a stick. Our theater group would lead charades, and *Name That Tune* would be played with a local musician.

Until Saturday, the area was fenced off. I glanced around. Everything was as we'd left it, so The Colonel and I strolled over to the cluster of tents I'd named Santa's Workshop. My best friend Connie had helped me finalize the décor for the market, but the holidays were a busy time for her craft store, and she hadn't been able to assist me in setting up the event.

For my last job, I'd hired my brother Dewey, but after being cleared of murder, he'd managed to get a job as a watchman with Sentinel Security. I was happy to see him gainfully employed but it'd left me in a bind until college let out for the holidays, and Madison Ross had been looking for a project to keep her from dwelling on the death of her father.

Setting up the event had been a logistical nightmare; coordinating with rental companies, volunteers, vendors, and city officials as well as placing decorations. Madison had taken responsibility for the Reindeer Games and Santa's Workshop areas while I focused on the holiday hamlet and the town square. The bonfire had been assembled by the fire department.

Looking around Santa's Workshop was firsthand proof that I'd been right to hire Madison. I'd known her since she worked as a barista at the Split Bean; we'd bonded over a mutual love of dogs and her desire to become a cop, but I'd given her the job because of her no-nonsense management style and ability to keep the wheels on the proverbial bus. Sympathy was also a factor in my decision; I knew what it was like to lose a father without warning.

CAROLERS AND CORPSES

Madison was also active in a local sewing guild and had convinced them to participate in the market. That club had brought others, and now Santa's Workshop had craft booths selling handcrafted items along with offering free tutorials and projects for kids of all ages. Its appeal rivaled the Reindeer Games.

Everything looked to be running smoothly. My eyes widened as I caught sight of Valentina DeMarco assisting at one of the craft tables run by the Saint Cecelia's by the Sea church. Her black leggings, knee high boots, and blue and gold Christmas sweater were a far cry from the Italian suits she usually wore, and her long black hair was pulled into a low ponytail instead of a chignon. I'd never seen the elegant CFO of the DeMarco Canning Company so animated or relaxed.

Valentina was manning the children's face painting table and she'd gotten into the spirit of the event by transforming her own. Cobalt blue makeup covered her, neck to jawline. The same shade of blue had been applied around both eyes, ending in a point on either side of her nose. Swaths of teal were blended with the cobalt to form a mask, and the medallion shapes of peacock feathers were drawn on her forehead in the same shades of teal, cobalt, and gold. With her dark eyes and olive skin the effect was stunning.

A small, chubby-cheeked boy pulled himself into the chair and pointed to the image he wanted painted onto his face. Valentina smiled and teased as she quickly transformed the little boy into a tiger. Her artistic talent was obvious, and I couldn't help but wonder what she'd have become if she hadn't been born a DeMarco; the calm, cool, and collected financial officer of a multimillion-dollar company was at odds with the whimsical woman I was watching.

The Colonel and I hung out a few minutes longer, observing the various tutorials on offer and doing a bit of window shopping when I could get close enough to a table. My bulldog drew attention, particularly that of children, and the main thoroughfare was jam packed with short humans, making me reluctant to go further into workshop. "C'mon, buddy, let's go around."

Intent on charming ice cream from a toddler, it took me three tries before The Colonel acquiesced. We walked around behind the tents and exited at the end of the workshop, next to the Sew Creative craft table.

I needn't have bothered taking the longer way around, the crowd of families and kids I'd intended to avoid were all crowded around my assistant's booth and, judging by the off-colored

CAROLERS AND CORPSES

language and semi-hysterical shrieks, I was guessing a sudden interest in sewing wasn't the draw.

I winced as some particularly rough words floated on the breeze. The ages of the kids made the shouting fest doubly unacceptable. Intending to shut down whatever was transpiring, I pushed my way through the rubberneckers but gasped as my gaze fell upon the participants.

Clutching a piece of plaid fabric in one hand and punctuating her rant by waving a pair of silver scissors, my highly competent and imminently professional assistant was red faced and almost frothing at the mouth.

Eyes wide in a pale face and curly brown hair standing up at odd angles, Madison leaned across the folding table and shouted at a tall blonde wearing a skintight sweater dress.

"Liar! You were only with Daddy for his money!" Madison snorted. "He only changed his will because of your lies!"

The heavily made-up woman smirked and ran her hand down her side, resting it on her thrust out hip. "Your father adored me, and he was *lonely*." She arched a perfectly drawn brow. "I made Clay's last days *pleasurable*, why shouldn't I be compensated?"

"Look at her, she's no better than she ought to be."

I frowned and glanced over to find Gary Walston and Kay Emory beside me. "Who is she?"

Gary's jaw was working overtime as he aggressively chomped on his gum. His eyes were hard as he glared at the scene unfolding in front of us, but Kay steered her electric chair a bit closer to me and tipped her head toward the tent. "That's Brianna Bellamy Ross."

Kay glared in the blonde's direction. "A cheap floozy. I don't blame Madison for yelling at her; I'd do more than yell if she seduced my father and turned him against me."

"What?" My eyes widened. "Are you telling me Clayton and Madison weren't speaking?"

Kay's chin went up and she gave a sharp nod.

I shook my head and tried to reconcile that with what I knew of the Ross family. Emma Ross had died of cancer when Madison was in middle school. Clayton had stepped up and been both mother and father.

Madison had worshipped her dad, and Clayton thought the sun rose and set with his daughter. They were a loving family, and I couldn't believe one woman had been able to come between them. I said as much, and Kay smirked.

"Morals of an alley cat but there is no denying she's beautiful, if you like the cheap, plastic, bimbo look."

Dressed in a short, body-con dress of kelly green, the new Mrs. Ross was endowed with curves in all the right places. From Kay's insinuations, I assumed her large and semi-exposed *attributes* were fake.

A glance at the long blonde tresses made me wonder if they were also not standard issue. I murmured my suspicions and was rewarded with more details of the bombshell's behaviors and beauty secrets than I ever wished to know.

"I can't believe you don't know her!" Kay rolled her eyes. "Do you watch *any* television?" She didn't wait for my reply. "I thought everyone had heard of Brianna Bellamy and her infamous sex tape! It rocketed her back into the spotlight when her singing career fizzled. Then she got that reality TV show ... nothing? Not ringing any bells?"

I chuckled. "Nope, sorry. I'm at least twenty years out of date music wise and we don't have cable. The only shows I watch are over a decade old." I shrugged. "No interest in the exploitive stuff that passes for television now."

"Unbelievable." She shrugged. "But in this case, you didn't miss anything. She went off to Hollywood and there was talk that she would be starring in that big blockbuster action-hero movie." She snorted. "All of a sudden it was announced that another actress got the part. Right after that Brianna moved into the house on Pineview Way and within a month she had her claws into Clayton Ross."

Kay's gossip went in one ear and out the other, I was too busy watching my assistant. Madison had a white-knuckled grip on the edge of the table and her expression said she was close to the end of her tether.

Brianna Bellamy Ross's face was set in a bland mask of haughty disdain, though the way she fidgeted with the gold scarf draped around her neck gave away her agitation.

Madison's face paled and her lower lip trembled. Her voice was strangled from suppressed emotions. "You caused hard feelings between me and my dad—"

"Oh please, that's on you." Brianna tossed the end of her scarf over her shoulder and pointed at Madison with a perfectly shaped red and white striped fingernail. "What did you expect your father to do when you *lied* about his wife?"

"Some *wife*." Madison hissed and her eyes narrowed to slits. "I saw you with Caleb!"

Brianna pouted. "A girl's got to a have a little fun."

CAROLERS AND CORPSES

Madison's eyes bulged and her mouth opened and closed like a fish out of water. She swallowed convulsively. "First my father and then my fiancée! You, you gold-digging whor—"

"*Darling*," Brianna quirked a brow. "Is that anyway to talk to your stepmother?" Her painted lips quirked into a smirk. "Relax, you can have the fiancée back,"—her nose wrinkled as she gave a mock shudder— "but maybe buy him an instruction manual before your wedding night."

A vein in Madison's forehead throbbed, and I worried she'd have a stroke. Her stepmother blithely carried on her verbal abuse.

"And, as for money, your college is paid for and, according to your father's will, you get everything when I die." She turned to walk away and then looked back over her shoulder, waving her ring finger so that all eyes were drawn to the large diamond nestled there. She smiled and mocked. "If there's anything left …"

"You hateful witch!" Madison ran around the table and grabbed Brianna's arm. "That ring belonged to my mother!"

"And now it's mine." Brianna laughed and shook off Madison's hold. Her heavily made-up eyes gleamed with malice as she flashed a cold smile. "Didn't you ever wonder why your father left everything to me?"

"You tricked him! Daddy would never have—"

"Tricked? Poor, deluded Madison." Brianna's lips turned down in a fake moue of sympathy as she shook her head. "Your father often told me what a burden it'd been to raise you."

"Liar! My father never said—"

"Oh, but he did!" She turned and started to walk away, "He also resented your mother—ah!"

A collective gasp rose above the din as Madison leapt at Brianna's back and grabbed the ends of her dangling scarf. "Shut up, you filthy—"

"Help! She's strangling me ... someone call the police!"

"Right, that's enough!" I handed The Colonel's leash to Gary and pushed my way through the crowd. "Madison! Have you lost your mind?"

Prying her fingers from the scarf, I dragged my assistant away as she and Brianna continued to hurl invectives.

"She assaulted me! You're all witnesses! Did someone video it? I'll see you in court, you crazy bitc—"

"Keep running your mouth you filthy tramp! Give me half a chance and I'll shut you up permanently and—"

CAROLERS AND CORPSES

"Madison!" Panting like she'd run a mile; her eyes were wild and not quite focused. I shook the younger woman until her mouth snapped closed and she met my gaze. "Take a deep breath."

Half turning, I hollered. "Ms. Ross, you need to leave." Brianna Bellamy Ross tossed her head and sneered but another hard look from me and she stalked off.

Turning back to Madison, I waited to speak until her breathing had evened out. "Madison, I know you're hurting but what you just did is assault! You'll be lucky if she doesn't file charges. You can't be a police officer with a conviction." My usually levelheaded assistant made no comment, merely glaring at the spot where Brianna had been and muttering under her breath.

I managed to catch the words "daddy" and "money" before I gave up and nudged her toward the exit. "You need to calm down. If you think that woman somehow connived her way into inheriting from your father then get a lawyer, but you can't go around choking people."

Posture rigid and lips pressed into a firm line, it was clear she hadn't heard a word I said. I sighed. "Go home, Maddie."

"I don't have a home, Holly!"

I blinked as Madison turned blazing eyes on me. "That vile woman stole it and I hope she dies!" She stomped off toward the bonfire area.

"Madison, you can't get through that way!" I yelled at her retreating back. "The gates to the parking area are locked. You'll have to go around—"

"I have a key." She hollered over her shoulder, never breaking stride.

Once she disappeared into the shadows, I returned to the workshop booths. Kay Emory rolled up accompanied by Gary. He handed me The Colonel's leash as I was contemplating going after Madison; something told me she shouldn't be left alone.

"I hope she's just going to cool off…"

Deep in thought, I frowned down at Kay. "Huh? She needs to go home and *sleep* it off. She could have hurt Brianna!"

Kay shrugged. "She deserved it."

"Kay!"

"Well, she does! Everyone hates her, Holly."

I glanced at Gary and found him nodding his head in agreement. My brows rose, the woman really hadn't ingratiated herself with the islanders!

"Well, that may be but Maddie's better off away from here tonight. "

Gary cleared his throat. "Madison is on the causeway committee ..."

Kay gasped. "That's right! We need her to take a turn in the booth!" She dug into her bag and pulled out a cell phone. "I'll just call and remind her."

"Better if you replace her, Kay."

"But Holly, it'll mess up the rotation! "

My leg was protesting in earnest and if The Colonel pawing at Kay's festive holiday leggings was any indication, he was getting anxious. It was time to head home. I waved, ignoring her continued arguments. "Have a good night, Kay."

She huffed and spun her chair around, yammering at Gary as they walked back toward Santa's Workshop. Turning to leave, I noticed Valentina DeMarco and a woman dressed as an elf that I thought was Felicity Simms enter into a heated discussion with Gary and Kay.

The way that they pointed toward the sewing booth left no doubt they were rehashing the scene we'd just witnessed and, being Sanctuary Bay, no doubt tongues would be wagging all over town before morning.

The crowd thinned out as we approached the Christmas tree. We were strolling along when The Colonel picked up the scent of something, probably food, and jerked me into a trot.

"Hey, boy, heel!" I tightened my grip on his lead and gave a sharp tug, but a bulldog on the trail was a tough beast to dissuade. Pulled through the field, I struggled to keep his pace and avoid running into other visitors.

I tried once again to rein in The Colonel but that broke my concentration and in short order, I'd walked into someone's back.

"Oh my gosh, I'm so sorry! Are you hurt?"

"Hello Deputy Daye."

I gulped and stumbled backwards as Roland Dupree, father of the young man I'd shot and killed while serving in the Noble County Sheriff's Department, turned to face me. He held my gaze but said nothing.

Uncomfortable, I looked down, absently noting he was wearing a pair of dirty tennis shoes and workout pants. Desperate to chase away thoughts of the shooting, my mind latched on to the oddity of his appearance.

Our paths had crossed over the years, whether at charity functions or various dinners and parties my husband had dragged me

CAROLERS AND CORPSES

to. As a personal injury attorney, Roland Dupree was famous throughout the Lowcountry, and he'd always looked like he stepped from the pages of a gentlemen's magazine.

Custom suits, gold watches, and monogrammed cufflinks; he'd oozed wealth and power, but he was a shell of that man now. I glanced at his face and stifled a gasp. Aside from the ratty clothing, his complexion was ashen, and a day's growth of hair dotted his cheeks and chin.

Stunned as I was by his unkempt appearance, it was the hollow, vacant look in his brown eyes that put a lump in my throat. My palms started to sweat. I struggled for words. "I ... er, Roland I ..."

The social niceties drummed into me by Mama kept running through my head but, throat drier than the Sahara, I couldn't make a sound. Besides, *I'm sorry for your loss. I'm sorry I killed your son*; What was the appropriate platitude in such a situation? Shawn Dupree was dead by my hand ...

Without warning a vision of that fateful night at the hunting camp rose in my mind.

The lights are blinding, I shade my eyes and try to figure out what is lying in the road. A deer? No ... the hair on the back of my neck stands on end, I raise my gun hand above the car door, finger inching toward the trigger—

Roland touched my arm and cleared his throat, pulling me back from the abyss of my memories. My stomach rolled as our gazes collided.

He opened his mouth to speak, and my heart kicked into overdrive. Civilized discourse dictated I should express some remorse for killing his son, only I realized with a start that I felt no guilt or shame; in fact, I felt nothing. Bile rose in my throat and my heartbeat pounded in my ears ... I needed-Oh, God, I couldn't—

Without thought, I pivoted around Dupree and started to hobble away as fast as my bum leg could manage, dragging The Colonel toward the parking lot like the hounds of hell were nipping at my heels.

Chapter Three

The headlights create halos of color across my field of vision, it's impossible to define what is up ahead. I slow the cruiser to a crawl and lean forward over the steering wheel but it's no use, I see nothing but the pickup truck blocking the road and blobs of color that might be people or animals.

Car in park, I stare through the windshield. There'd been someone standing beside the truck, I *know* I saw them. My chest is tight, I force myself to take a deep breath and I wipe my clammy hands on my pant legs.

A look to the left and then right but the shadows are too deep, and there is no sign of movement. My skin crawls, every instinct says flee ... what is that laying in the road? I slide my gun from its holster, open the car door, and slowly stand.

What's that? I cock my head and try to hear above the ticking of the engine. There it is again, music? A radio? Where is it? A rustling in the leaves, a twig snaps, I turn my head...BAM! My ears are ringing, and my leg is on fire. I stumble, my leg goes out from under me, my head connects with the door jamb, everything goes dark.

The roar of an engine turning over rouses me. The ground is hard, something is digging into my lower back. My leg throbs, I whimper and then scream as my gaze connects with...

"Ahh!" Chest heaving, breaths coming in short bursts, I jack-knifed up in bed. What had I seen and what was that noise? I jumped as the ringtone I'd assigned to my brother broke the silence.

Great, just what I needed. My hand trembled as I reached for the phone. "Yeah, Dewey, what is it?" I swallowed hard and shoved my damp hair away from my forehead.

CAROLERS AND CORPSES

"You need to get down here, Holly! I don't know what it... well it's a hand but I ain't—"

"Dewey, slow down. I'm not awake enough." Ignoring his huff, I blinked and scrubbed at my eyes. A few deep breaths and my heart was on its way to beating properly, though I was still sweaty, and my hands were shaking.

I sat up and tried to make sense of my brother's convoluted conversation. "Okay, what is... no, start with where you are."

Dewey huffed again. "I'm working! At the holiday market." He added when I failed to respond. "You need to get down here!"

I reached for my cane and rose, fumbling into my clothes while juggling the phone against my ear with my shoulder. "Okay but what is going on? Why can't you handle it?"

"I don't know what to do! Nothing in the security guard training manual about finding a hand under the snow!"

His comment brought me fully awake with a thump. "A hand? Whose hand? Is it connected to someone? Dewey, why didn't you call the paramedics?"

"I don't know who it belongs to. Pretty red nails so I'm guessin' it's a woman."

"You think a woman is lying under the snow? Where? Is she hurt? Hang up and call 911!" I grabbed a jacket and stared down at The Colonel, snug in his bed and resolutely not looking at me.

I debated not taking him, but it was after one in the morning and Lord only knew what mess I was heading into or how long it'd take to fix it; The Colonel wouldn't thank me for leaving him to beg breakfast from Mama; she was stingy with the kibble.

Ignoring Dewey's continued rambling in my ear, I nudged the dog bed with the tip of my cane. "Come on, buddy, up an at 'em."

An eye opened to half-mast, and a snuffled grunt was The Colonel's reply. "Colonel, treat?" I stepped back as my pudgy friend scrambled out of his bed, stretched, and then trotted to the door. Tail wagging, he looked over his shoulder as I approached. "Okay, okay, I'm coming."

Halfway down the stairs, Dewey finally ran out of steam, allowing me to get a word edgewise. "You're standing there talking my ear off when you should be calling the police. Did you at least check for a pulse?" I dug into the biscuit canister, handed one to The Colonel, and pocketed more; I sensed it was going to be a long morning that would require more bribery at some point.

"No, I didn't check cuz I ain't touchin' her ..." Dewey's voice trailed off and I could hear the murmur of voices in the background.

"Dewey! What is goin'—"

"Look, you comin' or not?"

"Oh for the love of ... I'll be there quick as I can."

My brother launched into a convoluted story detailing how he'd found the woman, or a woman's hand anyway. Setting the phone on speaker, I tuned Dewey out and stooped to boost The Colonel into my International Scout.

Recently serviced after a transmission failure, my father's old truck roared to life without a hitch and in minutes I was barreling down an empty Bay Street towards Goodwin Park.

A forty-something-year-old truck was not equipped with hands-free communication, but that didn't keep my brother from getting his point across; he merely hollered loud enough to make my phone speaker rattle.

"... and leave me out of it when you call."

I rolled my eyes and shifted gears. "Dewey ..." Several pithy remarks sprang to mind but, in the end, I merely told him I'd be in the parking lot in under ten minutes and cut the call.

As irritated as I was with my brother, I understood his reluctance to place the emergency call. The lead detective for the Noble County Sheriff's Department was an arrogant man more interested in rising in rank than fighting crime. He was quick to make a case on the flimsiest of circumstantial evidence; Dewey had learned that the hard way.

The parking lot was fuller than I'd anticipated. The special effects company truck and Dewey's car were expected but that left half a dozen vehicles scattered around the lot.

I'd given the Gray's Island Community Choir permission to hold a rehearsal after hours, but hadn't realized so many would be attending, and I'd have thought they'd be finished long before.

My eyes narrowed as I spotted an older man sitting behind the wheel of a silver sedan. What was he doing in the parking lot at such an early hour? My cop instincts prodded me to inquire but the desperation in Dewey's voice kept me moving.

My leg was throbbing, reminding me that it hadn't received nearly enough down time. The rest of my body was also protesting being pulled from a warm bed so, without a second thought, I swung the Scout onto the grass next to the entrance gates and pulled the emergency brake.

Reaching into the glove box for a flashlight, I attempted to wake my dog up. "Come on, Colonel, time to go." Man's best friend was giving me evil eyes. "I know it's cold. Blame it on Dewey."

The Colonel shifted in his seat, tucking his nose under his paw and doing a great job of ignoring me until I reached into my pocket and pulled out a handful of treats.

Brown eyes opened wide, and his nub of a tail started wagging as he watched me tuck the bones back into my jacket pocket. "You'd eat until you popped if I let you!" I chuckled and hauled his chubby butt out of the truck, promising him a biscuit when we found my brother.

The promise of food got my bulldog moving and in minutes we were striding toward the town Christmas tree. Shifting from foot to foot and looking pale, Dewey was surrounded by a small crowd of angry people all talking at once.

On sight of my brother, The Colonel tugged the leash out of my hand and barreled through all obstacles to reach his goal and, once his target was achieved, he proceeded to bark his head off. I stood back and assessed the chaos.

Kay seemed to be the spokeswoman for the group. Gary was adding his two cents while Maddie and Valentina DeMarco stood behind them, their disapproval obvious by the scowls on their faces.

Standing to the right of Kay was a sharp dressed man I'd never seen before and just behind him were what I assumed to be the rest of the carolers. Felicity Simms was shaking her finger at Dewey while Vincente DeMarco, twin to Valentina, stood beside her trying to get a word in edgewise.

My eyes widened as I realized who else was part of the crowd—Roland Dupree! I gulped as scenes from my earlier nightmare reared their head. No! I wasn't going there!

Pushing everything else from my mind, I walked around the frenzied pack of people and came up behind my brother. "All right everyone let's just simmer down." I snapped my fingers and frowned at The Colonel. "That goes for you too!"

The humans responded to my cop tone, but it took another biscuit to quiet my bulldog. With everyone still fuming but thankfully quiet, I turned my attention to Dewey.

"Now then, what did you drag me out of bed for?"

"Bed! I'll be lucky to see mine!"

"Now will you tell us why we're being kept here?"

"You have no right to keep us."

"That crazy brother of yours thinks he can make me stay ..."

"Do you know who I am? I'll speak to the mayor about ..."

My question reignited the verbal free for all. My brother backed away as the raised voices bombarded me. After trying to respond to the rapid-fire questions while also asking a few of my own I reached the limit of my patience.

Thumb and index finger between my lips, I managed to whistle. The piercing sound startled everyone to silence.

"Finally."

Kay started to speak, and I put my finger up. "Just a second, Kay." I turned to Dewey. "Why'd you tell all of these people to stay?"

Dewey gulped. "Uh, figured the cops would want to talk to 'em."

"Police! What's going on?"

"We were just here to practice; the director is gone and—"

"Now listen here, I am a respected business—"

"What's happened? Why are the cops coming?"

Great, they were all flapping their gums again. Rolling my eyes, I ignored the muddle of questions being tossed at me and crossed to Dewey. "Show me what you found."

Leaving the others squawking their indignation, we took the main path across the park. Dewey was again chattering about his reasons for not calling the cops. I half listened, but I was focused on keeping The Colonel out of the mud puddles scattered along the route while my mind started listing all the tasks I'd need to accomplish now that my day seemed to have started.

Skirting around another spot of standing water zeroed my focus onto the paths. The concrete was darker, suggesting the entire area had been soaked recently, and in numerous spots there were puddles a couple of inches deep.

A few sets of muddy footprints and some narrow tracks marred the path, but I was more concerned with why it was wet rather than the state of someone's shoes.

The sprinklers must have come on and the parks and rec people would need to be reminded of their promise to cut them off for the week. That task could be delegated to Madison, along with contacting the Sweetly Southern vendor about their booth; I'd noticed their banner had come loose.

CAROLERS AND CORPSES

I'd need to call Connie about the latest changes to the centerpieces I'd ordered for the Osprey Point Ladies Auxiliary, but Madison had the rest of that event under control. I snorted. God save me from women with too much time on their hands!

The Osprey Point New Year's Eve celebration notwithstanding, my new business' calendar was empty until mid-January; a fact I wasn't at all sorry about. Starting *CoaStyle* had been Connie's idea, and when I'd dragged my feet, she'd simply charged ahead and secured an office next to Glitter and Garlands Craft shop for me. Between Connie and Mayor Tomlin, I hadn't lacked clients since opening a month ago.

"You gonna go look? She ain't getting' any younger."

My gaze flew to Dewey. Lost in thought, I'd not noticed that we'd reached the end of the sidewalk. My brother had stepped off the path, presumably so that I could continue without him, but it left him standing in a pile of fake snow up to his knees.

"Dewey, you're gonna wreck the snow before anyone gets here!"

He shook his head. "Nah, this stuff doesn't melt like what they used yesterday." He bent over and grabbed a handful of faux snow. "Look, it's mostly this cloth. Then they put powder down and spray it all with water. It was cool watching it puff up."

The expression on my face must have been sufficient to disclose my annoyance because Dewey rolled his eyes and moved back onto the path. "Happy now...oh, crud look at my pants!"

A glance at his pant legs showed a clear line where the fake snow had touched; it reminded me of the soap ring left in a bathtub. Hiding my smirk, I headed across the lawn, leaving Dewey muttering about his ruined uniform.

Though he'd refused to accompany me, my brother had given detailed directions; whomever was lying in the snow, and Dewey hadn't convinced me there actually was a person in the snow, but whatever he'd seen, it was between the sewing club's tent and the bouncy castle.

Rounding the corner in Santa's Workshop, I waved my flashlight over the area, stopping as something glittered in a fake snow drift.

Unable to tell what it was, I glanced to the right of it and gulped. Four red spots, that based on Dewey's ramblings, I suspected were long fingernails, protruded from a snow drift. Nothing else was visible, though humps in the snow suggested the hand was attached to its owner, a small mercy under the circumstances.

CAROLERS AND CORPSES

Owing apologies to Dewey, I bit my lip. Who was under that snow blanket?

Mouth dry, I pulled out my phone, pressing the numbers for 911. My finger hovered as I considered connecting the call. Dispatch would have questions I couldn't answer. I slipped the phone back into my pocket and moved closer.

Conscious of the area being a potential crime scene, I shortened The Colonel's leash and watched my step as I made my way forward. No snow had been laid behind the tents, but the grass was wet, and the ground squelched beneath my feet.

Stumbling over some deep ruts, I jumped back and promptly sank into a puddle of mud. What the—that wasn't caused by a sprinkler. Where had the water come from? I looked for the cause.

My brows rose as I spotted a green hose hanging from a reel that was mounted on the side of the brick building that housed the park's restrooms. Water was streaming from it at a slow but steady rate.

Water could tamper with evidence. I glanced at the snow drift, debating priorities, but whether it was a lone hand, or one attached to a body, it clearly wasn't going anywhere. I took a few steps toward the hose, but The Colonel had other ideas.

"Hey boy, what are you after?" My arm was nearly wrenched from its socket as The Colonel gave another sharp tug. Sighing, I allowed him to lead me toward whatever he'd set his sights upon and in seconds I was struggling to pull a piece of red and green plaid fabric from his jowls.

Once free, I realized the fabric was the dog coat I'd commissioned Madison to make for my little buddy. A quick inspection showed it was damp but none the worse for wear after a tussle with The Colonel. Tucking it into my back pocket, I pondered how the dog coat had come to be on the grass around the corner from the sewing booth.

When last seen, my assistant had been clutching it in her fist as she screeched at her stepmother. The Colonel's detour had brought me closer to the red spots peeping out of the snow drift.

As suspected, they were fingernails, long, well-shaped nails painted to resemble candy canes. Like the dog coat, I'd seen that nail art before ...

Mouth dry as dust, I swallowed hard and wiggled my jacket's sleeve down until it covered my hand. Pressing the send button on my phone, I then used my covered hand to push the faux snow aside and roll the hand's owner over. I sucked in a breath.

CAROLERS AND CORPSES

"911, what's your emergency?"

I rose and took a few steps back. "This is Holly Daye. I'm at Goodwin Park and I've found a woman lying on the ground unresponsive."

I listened to dispatch's instructions with half an ear. As a former deputy sheriff, I could have recited it word for word; my time was better spent preserving the crime scene because I didn't need a coroner to tell me that Brianna Bellamy Ross had choked to death on a mouthful of expandable faux snow.

Chapter Four

The slam of the screen door roused me from sleep. A glance at the clock on my nightstand showed I'd only managed to grab a four-hour nap. Dang Dewey and his phone call!

Body protesting, I shook away sleepiness and swung my feet to the floor. It'd been well past daylight before the police had let us leave and I'd had an additional interrogation from Tate, though he'd been too busy directing removal of the body to keep me for long.

Regardless, between the nightmare, Dewey's phone call, and then the rigamarole of a crime scene, I'd had less than five hours of sleep and the last thing I wanted to do was leave the comfort of my bed. But word of Brianna Bellamy's death at the holiday market would soon be all over town and I needed to do some damage control.

A snort and snuffle from The Colonel suggested he was also less than enthused with rising from a warm bed. I leaned over to pat his head and my gaze fell upon the journal my therapist had given me.

Cursing my ingrained sense of duty, I picked it up and then looked around for an object with no emotional value. The DBT therapy I'd learned last month still made me feel silly, but I couldn't deny that it was working; my ability to be in Roland Dupree's vicinity for several hours while the police processed the scene was proof.

Grabbing a bottle of hand lotion, I sat cross-legged on the bed and began the DBT ritual I'd established. Deep breath in, hold, then out; rinse and repeat a couple of times until I relaxed, and my mind was calm. Releasing one last deep breath, I opened the blue leather journal and began to observe my chosen object.

The lotion bottle is white, the product name is in bold, dark blue ink and there is smaller text in yellow. There is a swishy scrolled line in dark gold followed by an outline of a hand. My concentration wavered as an image of Brianna Bellamy's stiff, slightly blue, and lifeless hand rose in my mind.

After calling 911 I'd listened with half an ear to the standard instructions as I tried to secure the scene. Water from the leaking hose had filled the ruts I'd tripped over earlier, and the overflow was creeping toward the body, so I picked my way across the muddy lawn and cut it off. While crossing the short distance, I'd found items of possible evidence, not that Detective Brannon had been interested.

Hours later, our conversation still managed to send my blood pressure soaring.

"A leaking hose and a whistle? That's evidence?" Brannon snorted and waved me away. "How about you leave this to the professionals, Daye?"

Swallowing a few choice words, I pinned a smile to my face and tried again to get the detective for Noble County to use what God gave him, or perhaps that was the problem my snide inner self offered. When God was handing out brains, Detective Joe Brannon thought He'd said trains and asked for a slow one.

CAROLERS AND CORPSES

Trying not to laugh, I pointed at the item I'd carefully picked up with my jacket covered hand and set on one of Santa's Workshop tables. "I appreciate you're a trained investigator, Detective"—being conciliatory nearly choked me but I continued—"however, I found the whistle on the concrete below the spigot handle. What if the killer dropped—"

"Oh, come on, Daye, use your head," he rolled his eyes and muttered, "if you have one."

Gritting my teeth, I ignored his insult and tried again to press my point. "This could be nothing but—"

"Nothing is right!" Brannon huffed and turned to speak with a uniformed officer.

Tapping my foot and dismissing one snarky reply to Brannon after another, I watched the forensic techs comb the area until Brannon again gifted me with his special brand of logic.

"Even if the killer, and I use that word loosely because we don't know if she *was* murdered yet, but *if* it ends up being murder, that garbage you found could have come from anyone. We aren't wasting county resources testing junk in the forensics lab, especially when they've been sitting out for anyone to contaminate!"

My ability to remain civil was hanging by a thread but I gave it one last shot. "Detective, the victim's throat is bulging from the expandable powdered snow streaming from her mouth. Odds are good someone else forced that stuff into her mouth and then used the hose to activate it." I cocked an eyebrow. "Or are you really trying to tell me she swallowed that powder on purpose?"

Brannon glared at me. "Of course, she didn't but maybe it was an accident. Either way, we're done here. The coroner will determine cause of death."

He turned to walk away and, much as I didn't want to engage him further, I couldn't stand by and watch him wreck a crime scene. "Brannon! If you're going to ignore the whistle I found, at least have forensics examine the holes in the snow."

"What?" He stalked back and looked down his nose at me. "You want me to expend resources on holes in fake snow?" He snorted. "You've lost the plot, Daye!"

That did it. Raising my voice to be heard above the safety beep as the coroner's van was backed into the alley between tents, I loosened the reins on my temper. "Oh really. So, you're just going to ignore evidence that someone was standing right next to the body? Not even going to take pictures or get plaster casts?"

Brannon smirked. "So now you're a forensics expert *and* a detective?" He snorted and shook his head. "You civilians kill me. For your information, those holes could have been made by anyone, at any time, and I'm not wasting mine taking casts for some random person's footprints!"

God save me from fools and blowhards! I took a deep breath before pointing out a few home truths. "Detective, that snow was just put down a few hours ago, no way those holes are—"

"Enough!" Brannon's mouth snapped shut and a nerve twitched in his cheek. "You hard of hearing or do you get off on looking stupid? I just said we are not wasting taxpayer's—" His eyes widened as a local TV news reporter called out a greeting.

With a murmured "stay out of this, Daye", Brannon pasted a smarmy smile onto his face and strolled over to the police cordon to schmooze the reporter.

Yipping dogs followed by a whine from The Colonel drew my attention back to the present. I pushed aside the memories of my frustrating conversation with Detective Brannon and closed my therapy journal. Throwing on a pair of jeans and a sweater, I took The Colonel downstairs, fed him a light brunch, and then walked out onto the front porch to find Mama entertaining her best friend, Maybelle Everette.

Miss Maybelle, along with being the aunt of my friend and former boss, was an obsessive dog lover. A few months before the shooting that ended my career, Maybelle's prize-winning and heavily pregnant Pomeranian had been dognapped and I'd been charged with finding the thieves.

I'd solved the case and returned Coco to the bosom of her loving owner and adopted The Colonel when his owners couldn't be located.

Coco had gone on to have three puppies, and Miss Maybelle, considering me an honorary aunt, never failed to bring the three hellions when she visited—much to the chagrin of The Colonel. I stifled a laugh as Winkin', Blinkin', and Nod pounced on my buddy as soon as he set his paws onto the porch.

"Oh, isn't that the sweetest thing?" Deaf as a post and too vain to wear a hearing aid, Miss Maybelle pronounced her observation loud enough to rouse the neighbors.

"It is! The Colonel just loves to play with the babies."

My mother was delusional or completely ignorant of dog body language because my poor bully was doing his best to avoid Coco's terrible toddlers, going so far as to wedge his pudgy butt under a chair. I patted his head and distracted the puppies with treats. No fool, The Colonel saw his chance and scrambled down the steps and out into the yard.

CAROLERS AND CORPSES

About to make a similar escape, I was brought up short as something Maybelle said caught my attention. Standing on the top step, I turned and waited for a break in the women's conversation.

"Miss Maybelle, did you just say reporters are camped out in front of the sheriff's department?"

Her gray curls danced as she energetically bobbed her head. "I did!" She clasped her hands in front of her and leaned toward me, eager to add another person to the gossip circle. "Bernice Ziggler drove by this morning on her way to the senior center—"

"Oh! That reminds me!" Mama helped herself to a chocolate donut. "Have you noticed how trim Bernice is lately? I really think we should go to those Roomba classes with her, Maybelle."

Maybelle frowned. "Is that what she's doing at the center? I thought she was learning to dance."

"Ms. Bernice *is* exercising by dancing, Miss Maybelle, and it's Zumba, Mama. Roomba is the robot cleaner...never mind." I shook my head, irritated that I'd let myself get distracted. "Why are there reporters at the police station, Miss Maybelle?"

She blinked and gave me a blank stare for a second. "What? Oh! Well, like I was saying, Bernice was on her way to the—"

"Yes ma'am, to the senior center and she saw the reporters, but why are they there?"

Mama frowned at me. "She was getting to that, Holly Marie!" She pursed her lips. "So impatient. Finish your story, Maybelle."

Maybelle's gaze shifted from me to Mama like she was watching a tennis match. I nodded and gave her an encouraging smile and after a few more nervous glances she continued.

"Well, as I was sayin', Bernice was passing by and saw all of those news vans and such." Eyes wide, she looked at Mama. "Bernice said one of the trucks had the Legal News Network logo on it. Effie, do you think Grace Neely will come?"

Mama's face lit up and she clasped her hands to her chest as if ready to pray. "Oh, surely not?" Mama turned her gaze toward me. "What do you think, Holly Marie? Will the news people send Grace Neely?"

My mother never missed an episode of Grace Neely and, if Maybelle's excited chatter was anything to go by, the other old ladies in Mama's circle were equally obsessed with watching the Legal News Network. Their addiction to the Neely woman's show was a mystery to me.

A former prosecutor, Neely had made a name for herself by offering blow-by-blow commentary on prominent court trials and police investigations. She was known for blunt speaking and ruthless tactics in pursuit of a story.

Along with her chosen topics, it was her abrasive personality that turned me off and, though she claimed Southern heritage, her strident, and to my ear forced, accent grated on my last nerve.

Refraining from rolling my eyes with great effort, my smile was tight as I replied. "Since I still don't know what has brought news outlets to Sanctuary Bay, I couldn't say, Mama."

Her brow furrowed. "Gracious, there's no call to be rude." Her eyes narrowed as she let her gaze roam over me. "Is your leg paining you? No matter, that's no reason to take it out on others." She shook her head and turned back to Maybelle, ignoring my muttered "yes ma'am."

"Wouldn't it be something if Ms. Neely did come here?" Mama fanned herself with her hand. "Oh, my goodness, I'm getting palpitations just imagining it."

"I know! It's so exciting." Maybelle's smile faded. "Though, a woman has died. Do you think our enthusiasm is a bit unseemly, Effie?"

Blood starting to boil, I gritted my teeth and started to demand an answer to the question I'd posed several long minutes ago when my phone rang, saving Mama and her bestie from the sharp edge of my tongue.

A glance at the caller ID caused my brow to furrow. Now what would Mayor Tomlin be calling me about? I walked to the other side of the porch and answered the call. "Hey Ms. Lou Lou, what can I do—"

"Oh, thank heavens! Get on down here on the double, Holly Marie, the whole town's gone crazy!"

Chapter Five

Running a gauntlet of journalists shouting questions, The Colonel and I squeezed through a gate half opened by a uniformed cop and strode further into the park. Once away from the bombarded entrance the holiday market was quiet as a tomb and a sense of déjà vu, followed by dread, enveloped me.

Passing through the holiday hamlet area, I was relieved to see my assistant hard at work repairing the booths I'd noticed were missing decorations. On a day where everything that could go wrong had, it was a relief to know Madison was staying on task.

I gave her a wave but didn't stop to chat. The mayor's frantic voice was still ringing in my ears, and I could understand her panic. It was after 3:00 p.m., the market should have been bustling with happy visitors perusing vendor stalls, learning crafts, playing games, or listening to Christmas stories and carols but the death of Brianna Bellamy had stopped all of that, and I wondered if the market would reopen at all.

All the work, all the money spent ... I was sorry a woman had lost her life but also a bit irritated. Why the holiday market? Everything was ruined and for what? I blew out a ragged breath; that had been an ugly thought and God didn't like ugly!

I continued to castigate myself until I caught up with Mayor Tomlin by the charity tents that lined the walkway behind the town Christmas tree.

Standing amidst a gaggle of fussing officials and city staffers, the mayor was fielding questions and soothing ruffled feathers. The Colonel and I stood well out of the fray, but Ms. Lou Lou made eye contact and wasted no time making a beeline toward us.

CAROLERS AND CORPSES

"Oh Holly Marie, thank goodness you're here!" She waved a hand at the people still clustered near the town Christmas tree. "Everyone's lost their collective minds!" Her lips pursed. "It's just like the Bellamy girl to cause trouble, even in death!"

My eyes widened at Ms. Lou Lou's words even as I silently forgave myself for similar thoughts. Had Brianna Bellamy really been such a thorn in people's side? I was dragged from my musings when the mayor leaned down and started talking to The Colonel.

"You are such a sweet boy, yes you are! Look what I bought for you!"

Ms. Lou Lou pulled a giant peanut butter stuffed bone from a bag. The Colonel snorted in excitement and settled on the grass with his treat. I rolled my eyes but refrained from commenting; as much as I thought half the town was trying to fatten up my already porky dog, he had been dragged all over creation since early morning.

"Now then,"—Mayor Tomlin dusted her hands off and met my gaze— "I've had vendors calling my office all morning, not to mention the merchant's association members and the press!" She continued her litany of woes for several minutes before arriving at a topic that I could do something about.

"... and the police have trampled the width and breadth of this park, just look at the state of the fake snow!"

I let my gaze roam and had to concede the artificial snow was looking a bit sad. I cleared my throat. "It could look better, but in fairness, it was never meant to be walked on this much ..."

"Not walked on." She huffed and put her hands on her hips. "If it can't stand up to traffic ... I'm not seeing the point of paying for something that can't be walked on."

"Well, the thing is, we'd assumed everyone would stay to the paths and I didn't have it applied to high traffic areas." Ms. Lou Lou looked perturbed, so I cut short my excuses. "I'll talk with the company when they come back to reapply it tonight."

She nodded and started to speak when a passel of uniformed officers ran past us. "What on earth is it now?"

I shrugged and trailed after her as she set off in the direction the police had taken. A commotion on the backside of the vendor stalls guided our steps and in minutes we drew to a halt in front of the Sweetly Southern booth.

Someone had let the news crews through the gates, and they were jockeying for position and shouting questions as the officers, along with Detective Joe Brannon, surrounded someone inside the tent.

CAROLERS AND CORPSES

"What is the meaning of this?"

The Colonel and I followed Ms. Lou Lou as she pushed her way through the crowd. My eyes widened as I reached the mayor's side and saw my assistant flanked by two officers.

Nodding at the mayor, Joe Brannon finger combed his hair and straightened his tie before positioning himself so that the cameras caught his profile.

"Madison Ross, you're wanted for questioning in the murder of Brianna Bellamy Ross."

The bell over the door jingled as The Colonel and I walked into my best friend Connie's craft shop. Glitter and Garland was teeming with holiday shoppers and Connie was busy at the checkout counter. The Colonel tugged on his leash and whimpered until I relented and let him go to the bed and food bowl that Connie kept behind the counter for him.

Denied ranting to my friend and temper hanging by a thread, I prowled the store feigning interest in the lushly decorated Christmas trees Connie had scattered around while I burned off some of my rage. Lost in thought, and on my third trip around the shop, I nearly jumped out of my skin when a hand fell onto my shoulder. I spun around to find Connie tsking and shaking her head.

"What?" My brow furrowed. "What's that look for?"

She chuckled and started straightening items on a nearby table. "You're like a cat in a roomful of rocking chairs. What's the matter with you?"

I drew a deep breath. "I'm irritated, sorry." A glance around the shop revealed it was empty of customers. "Where did everybody go?"

Connie quirked a brow. "Last customer just left and it's closing time." She finished straightening and returned to the cash register to begin totaling receipts. Putting on her reading glasses, she grinned at me. "So, what has your tinsel tangled?"

I smirked at her joke and grabbed a broom before replying. "I was at the sheriff's department." I leaned over and swept under a display table, drawing glitter and dust bunnies into a pile. "Do you know what that fool Brannon did?"

Connie looked up from her paperwork. "Let me guess. It's something *other* than finding Brianna Bellamy's killer?"

"I wish!" I pushed the debris into a dustpan and then leaned on the broom handle. "No, for once Joe's on the ball." I snorted. "He's just playing in the wrong field!"

She gave me a puzzled frown and I explained. "He's taken Madison in for questioning!" I pursed my lips but couldn't contain my anger. "With her father gone, she has no one! Twenty-two years old and probably scared out of her wits."

"That's awful." Connie shook her head. "On what grounds?"

I told her about the very public argument between Madison and her stepmother.

"Oh my gosh, how lame! How is that enough to arrest someone?"

"Detained."

Connie shrugged. "Same thing."

It wasn't, but I didn't feel up to a lecture on legal procedures, so I let it slide. The bottom line was that Madison Ross was being held on suspicion of murder and, if Brannon had his way and could produce enough evidence to convince the DA, she'd soon be charged.

"It's Joe Brannon." I cocked my head and quirked a brow and Connie's eyes widened as she cottoned on to what I was implying.

"Oh, you are kidding me. Again?" She shook her head. "You'd think he would have learned after last time."

"Nope, and what's more he did it late in the day so she can't get an attorney!"

Connie sighed. "Of all the— that man is a menace!"

No reply was necessary from me on that score as I'd made my feelings about Joe Brannon known numerous times.

"So, what are you going to do?"

"Me? Nothing I *can* do."

Connie directed a pointed stare at me.

"No." I shook my head for added emphasis.

Holding my gaze, she tilted her head to the side and quirked an eyebrow.

"It's none of my business."

"You just said she has no one to support her and if Brannon thinks he's got his man, er girl ..." She shrugged. "You know he'll consider the case closed now."

Connie was right, not that I wished to admit it. Brannon was a one trick pony; he'd arrested my brother on the same flimsy excuse of an argument with the victim that he'd used with Madison.

To save Dewey, I'd had to find the real killer, but it'd been a fluke. I was not a trained investigator and had no business inserting myself into law enforcement matters. However, there were things I could do to help Madison Ross.

"If they charge her and Madison is granted bail, I'll put up the money."

My friend sniffed. "Commendable."

Her tone said it was anything but.

"Connie ..." I sighed. "I've already called the attorney that helped Dewey. Max Bernard did an excellent job keeping him out of prison."

"Not as much as you did!"

"I got lucky."

Connie's lips pursed, and one eyebrow was cocked. She continued to stare at me until I got fidgety and broke eye contact. "What else can I do?"

Connie looked at me over the top of her glasses. "I'm sure I don't know." She scooped up the receipts and walked to her office, leaving me to stew.

Without uttering a word, Connie made it clear that she *did* know what I should do and, much as I hated to admit it, I did too. For several minutes I argued with my conscious and ignored my friend's pointed looks.

I shouldn't get involved ... well, no more than I'd planned to and that wasn't much! Any decent person would help an orphaned girl get an attorney and ... I huffed. She was barely out of her teens! It was my Christian duty to offer assistance and support but that didn't mean ...

"Talk yourself into it yet?"

I glared at Connie, but she just smirked and went back to her bookkeeping.

"Fine." I groaned and rolled my eyes. "But if this thing goes pear shaped, I'm blaming you!"

Chapter Six

Hours later, sitting on the patio at Mario's Cucina waiting for Tate to arrive, I was still grumbling over Connie's badgering. That she was right only made it worse. What did I know about investigating?

Sure, I'd managed to find the killer of Megan Hearn and save Dewey from being put on trial for murder, but it'd been a combination of common sense and luck. An aberration and a necessity, I mentally conceded, because Brannon had made it clear he'd found his man.

Just like now, my pesky inner voice tossed out. I rolled my eyes and surrendered. Madison would be steam rolled into prison, or at least dragged through the courts, if I didn't get involved. I scowled. I couldn't deny she needed my help, but that didn't mean I was happy about it.

"Dare I ask what that drink did to you?"

My gaze rose to find Tate hovering beside the table, a teasing smile gracing his lips. I snorted and motioned to the chair across from mine.

He settled in. "So, you've just been sitting here arguing with your white wine?" He snickered.

"It was giving me lip."

He grinned. "That usually indicates someone has had one too many. Am I that late?"

Fighting a laugh, I rolled my eyes. "Stop it."

His smile was unrepentant. "I'm just saying ..."

With a shake of my head, I handed him the menu. "I haven't ordered yet, but I know what I want."

Tate nodded and studied the menu. We gave our orders to the server and then he leaned his elbows on the table and smiled.

"So, what's troubling you? Or do you always have stare downs with alcohol?"

I smirked. "Just fuming over Madison's detention."

Tate's eyebrows rose. "Funny you should mention that. It's the reason I was late." At my questioning glance, he continued. "Brannon was breathing down my neck for the autopsy report."

The server set a salad in front of me and a bowl of she-crab soup for Tate. Spearing a piece of lettuce onto my fork, I waited until we were alone to comment.

"Why am I not surprised?" The salad turned to ash in my mouth. I sighed and picked at the croutons and olives. "He's in a big rush to railroad Madison."

"Mmm." Tate swallowed a bite of soup. "Though, not sure what I found is going to help his cause."

"How so?"

"Just that, aside from the sewing scissors there is precious little physical evidence, and what there is doesn't point conclusively to Madison."

"What do you mean?" Lack of evidence was a good thing, at least where Madison was concerned. I tamped down on the hope rising within me.

Tate held my gaze for a minute. "Why do I get the feeling this isn't idle curiosity?"

My brows rose, though I refrained from answering.

He sighed and set his spoon down. "You're sticking your nose in again."

Bristling at his tone, I straightened my spine. "I have no choice, well according to Connie anyway."

His eyes narrowed. "This isn't your responsibility, Holly." I started to reply but he held up his hand. "No, hear me out, please. Dewey being charged and Brannon refusing to look for another culprit meant you had no choice, but I don't see how—"

"The same reasons apply, Tate." I pushed my salad plate toward the edge of the table and leaned forward to avoid being overheard. "I'm not going to pretend I like this, but Brannon is not competent ... no, that's not true. He's probably semi-capable of investigating, but you know what he's like, more concerned with rising through the ranks by playing politics than seeing justice done!"

The server placed our dinners on the table, halting our conversation. The Colonel scraped my leg with his fat paw, reminding me of his unspoken rule; when Holly ate, so did he.

CAROLERS AND CORPSES

Digging through my bag for the busy bone Mayor Tomlin had given him, it was several minutes before I turned my attention back to Tate. I braced for more arguing over my decision to investigate the murder of Brianna Bellamy but, to my shock, Tate had surrendered with nary a shot fired.

"I'm surprised you don't have a list of reasons I should mind my own business."

His brows rose. "Did I say that I didn't? You aren't in law enforcement anymore, you are still suffering from PTSD issues, and butting in almost got you killed."

"Okay, you've made your point, but—"

He held his hands up in surrender. "I could go on, but I won't." He reached across the table and squeezed my hand. "Just promise me you will be careful. No going off alone chasing down clues or—"

"Or going to deserted plantations in the middle of the night." I grinned because I knew I'd won. "Got it! Now, what did you find during the autopsy?"

Tate rolled his eyes. "You're incorrigible."

"Duly noted, now give!"

He chuckled and took the last bite of his baked rigatoni before satisfying my curiosity. "Mmm, that hit the spot. Now then, the results of the autopsy." He tipped his head toward me. "We found a receipt from Sushi Zen in her purse. From the time stamp, contents of her stomach, and witness statements, I was able to put her time of death between a quarter after midnight and one a.m."

"That makes sense. Dewey called me around 1:30, and it was probably another thirty minutes before he showed me where he'd found her."

Tate nodded. "Sorry to say, you're losing your touch."

I cocked my head to the side. "How so?"

"Your initial assumption as to cause of death was incorrect; Brianna Bellamy Ross did not choke to death on faux snow."

"Really? But it was packed in there so tightly her cheeks were puffed up and her throat was—"

"Uh-huh, and that *would* have cut off her airway, had she still needed to breathe."

My eyes widened. "You're saying she was already dead when someone stuffed the powder in her mouth and added water?"

"Yep, though I'm still waiting on the tox screen I'm fairly certain she wasn't breathing when the powder was placed in her mouth."

I frowned. "How do you know that?"

Tate shrugged. "No expandable snow found in her lungs and no signs of struggle." He quirked an eyebrow. "Hard to believe someone would willingly allow that stuff to be poured down their throat."

"True." Thinking of the gruesome death made me shiver. "What would you have found if she'd been awake and fought against her killer?"

"Eh, everyone is different but definitely bruising around the mouth and possibly fingermarks on the neck and jaw, since the killer would have had to forcibly hold the victim still."

Frowning, Tate cocked his head to the side and looked into the distance. "Thinking along those lines, I'd also expect to find some marks on the victim's hands and forearms, and the blue substance I did find isn't from defensive wounds."

"What was on her hand?"

The server brought our bill and Tate was preoccupied with filling out the charge slip for a few minutes. I sat back, thinking about what I'd seen when I found Brianna's body, red and white striped fingernails on a pale, vaguely blue hand.

"I noticed her hand was kinda blue, but I thought it was a normal part of being dead."

Tate snapped the leather folder closed and then met my gaze. "Not exactly. Pallor mortis is the first stage of death and causes a blueish tint to light skinned people, but this was different."

"How so?"

He rose and motioned for me to precede him out of the restaurant. Once on the sidewalk, Tate continued his explanation as he walked The Colonel and me to my truck.

"We aren't sure what the blue substance is, but it is slightly greasy and only on the palm and fingers of her right hand. I sent it off to the lab in Columbia."

We walked along Bay Street, me thinking about Brianna Bellamy and the predicament Madison found herself in and Tate chatting about New Year's Eve. I was only half listening until I heard the words Osprey Point. "I'm sorry, what about Osprey Point?"

Tate shook his head. "I should probably be offended that you weren't listening but ..." He started to say something, stopped, shook his head, and then began again. "You were thinking about this murder."

It wasn't a question, but I nodded anyway.

Tate sighed and dragged a hand through his hair. "You're about to get wrapped up in this case, aren't you?" When I didn't bother to reply, Tate rolled his eyes and muttered, "Jealous of a murder victim."

Refusing to touch his comment with a ten-foot pole, I changed the subject. "My mind was wandering, sorry. I heard something about New Year's but got confused when you jumped to talking about Osprey Point." I schooled my features and gave what I hoped was an apologetic smile. "Not sure what one has to do with the other."

Tate snorted. "The Osprey Point New Year's Eve party? The one that everyone in Sanctuary Bay wants to attend? The one you're decorating for? I was asking you to go with me, Holly."

My eyes widened. "Oh! Uh ... I missed that part." I mumbled something irrelevant and inane as my mind started running nineteen to a dozen in the wrong direction. He wanted me to attend the New Year's party on Osprey Point!

Tate was wrong in thinking I was decorating for the party; the ladies on the committee had purchased centerpieces and a few other props from me and Connie but I wasn't tasked with setting up the event. He was, however, right in saying everyone who was anyone longed for an invitation to the exclusive party held at the Lilycreek Luxury Resort.

While I'd been to Rose Island numerous times, I'd never had the chance to visit the gated community of Osprey Point or the resort it was built around. I'd be lying if I said the idea of seeing it didn't tempt me.

Lilycreek was a five-star resort built around the ruins of Barnwell plantation. There were three championship level golf courses, clay tennis courts, miles of unspoiled beach, a full-service spa, and the old plantation's gardens and outbuildings. It was the remains of Barnwell that I was most interested in, though I wouldn't turn my nose up on a day of pampering at the spa.

The trouble was, Rose Island was only accessible by boat and by default, a New Year's Eve party meant staying until at least midnight A boat ride late at night in the dead of winter wasn't a good idea, which meant we'd need to stay overnight and that was problematic. Would he expect us to share a room?

We were both adults, it shouldn't be this hard and yet, for me, it was. I liked Tate a lot, but I wasn't inclined to take our relationship beyond good friends that enjoyed dinner and similar types of dates. I wouldn't mind going to the party, but how to broach the subject of separate rooms without making myself look foolish?

CAROLERS AND CORPSES

Which left me with only one option. What could I say? How did I say no without hurting his feelings or worse, wreck our friendship! I gritted my teeth and avoided Tate's questioning gaze.

This was exactly why I'd resisted being anything more than casual friends! Less than two months ago, I'd relented and agreed to go out to dinner and now he was asking me to attend an event that would require an overnight stay! Oh, I was not ready for this.

Tate quirked an eyebrow and cleared his throat; he wanted an answer. "Um …" Mouth dry, I swallowed hard and prayed for inspiration. "That uh, that sounds like an uh …"

Tate sighed and his lips pressed into a firm line. "If you don't want to go just say so, Holly."

Oh great, now he was mad. This. This was why … I huffed. "No, it's not that! Um, it's just …" My eyes widened as my brain kicked in and gave me a way out, or at least a reprieve. "I need to check with Mama." I flashed him a rueful smile. "You know how she is. Let me make sure she hasn't already made plans."

His expression softened. "Sure, I understand, but I'll need to know by the end of the week so I can RSVP."

"Of course! I'll let you know. Um, guess I'd better get this spoiled pooch home." Unlocking the truck, I started to pick up The Colonel, but Tate beat me to it.

"Come on you little sack of spuds, up you go."

The Colonel turned around three times before settling himself onto the passenger seat with a huff. Smiling at Tate, I fastened my seat belt and started the truck. "Thanks for dinner." I snorted. "Probably my last bit of peace until Madison is off the hook."

The expected commiseration from Tate was not forthcoming, instead his smile faded and a concerned look crept into his eyes. "Holly …"

I braced for a lecture about minding my own business and leaving things to the professionals, but Tate was full of surprises.

"There's a medical conference I can't get out of, so I'll be in Charleston for a few days." His teeth worried at his lower lip. He started to speak then seemed to think better of it.

Before I could blink, Tate leaned over the windowsill and dropped a quick kiss onto my lips. "Try and stay out of trouble, at least until I'm here to bail you out."

Chapter Seven

Brannon's declaration that they had a person of interest had allowed the reopening of the holiday market and the Lowcountry weather did not disappoint.

Bright and balmy, it was a perfect day for strolling through the riverfront park for everyone but me; I was too busy worrying over who had killed Brianna Bellamy Ross.

Mama had convinced Ms. Maybelle to try the senior center's exercise class, which left breakfast up to me and, since my cooking skills weren't sufficient to scramble a decent egg, I fed The Colonel and then treated myself to breakfast at the Country Kitchen.

Well, that had been my plan but, arriving at the diner to find half the town had similar intentions, I reversed course and settled for a cup of coffee at the Split Bean and one of owner Bill Graves' decadent chocolate croissants.

Ordering anything at the Split Bean was a drawn-out process with The Colonel in tow as the baristas never missed an opportunity to pet and pamper him. With my order finally placed, I'd thought I could retreat to my usual table by the window for some quiet contemplation while I chased a sugar high, but it was not to be.

My rear end had no sooner connected with the wooden chair than first Wanda and then Bill Graves stopped by to question me on the predicament Madison Ross found herself in.

"I just don't know what the world is coming to!" Bill Graves shook his head and slid a plate across the table. "Try the sour cream coffee cake, it's a new recipe."

Bill and his amazing baking skills were a prime reason why I tried not to frequent his coffeehouse more than once a week. I'd lost a lot of weight after the shooting and Bill seemed determined to help me find it again. Still, I was happy to be a taste tester while he ranted about Sanctuary Bay's buffoon of a detective.

"Wanda and I are just sick over this, Holly! That poor girl. Any dang fool can see she wouldn't hurt a flea! Why, she was one of my best employees. Always on time, willing to work late or pick up extra shifts ..." He sighed and brushed some crumbs off the table. "This is gonna be a nightmare for all of us."

Unsure of what he meant and mouth full of cake, I cocked my head and frowned.

"Already had a group of reporters in this morning digging for dirt on Maddie, and most of them were from those cable networks." Bill scowled and thumped the table with his fist. "Bunch of vultures! Somehow they found out Madison used to work here."

My eyes widened and I set down my fork. "You're kidding! What kind of dirt can they possibly expect to find on a twenty-two-year-old kid?"

Bill's lips pressed into a firm line. "Asking about her dad marrying that woman. Was it true that Clayton had thrown Maddie out of the house after she accused Brianna of sleeping with her fiancée, and did I know if the rumors were true about that tramp inheriting Ross's fortune and leaving his daughter out in the cold?" He sniffed. "I sent them packing."

"Good. None of that is relevant to the crime. But Bill, why are they interested? Murder is rare in a small town like this but surely there is something happening around the country that should take precedence."

Bill snorted. "It's a slow news cycle I guess. Oh, and they kept going on about how Brianna Bellamy had been the winner of some talent search show?" He shrugged. "I'd never heard of her, but Felicity Simms swore that was the reason the Gray's Island council voted to make Bellamy the leader of their community choir."

He leaned across the table, eyes wide. "The group came in after rehearsals one night, minus their leader, and they weren't shy about how much they hated her! Felicity seemed to be the ringleader, as I recall." He laughed. "Said she couldn't carry a tune in a bucket outside of a studio but J.T. thought it'd look good and get them publicity before that state competition they're going to next spring. And you know what J.T. Minton wants, he gets."

Hmmm, my ears perked up at that tidbit. That Minton was involved didn't surprise me. The local developer and business

CAROLERS AND CORPSES

owner had his fingers in every pie. It also wasn't news that Felicity Simms had a beef with Brianna Bellamy.

I recalled what Kay Emory had said about Mrs. Simms being neighbors with Brianna. The relationship had been hostile from what I gathered, but I'd take that with a grain of salt because Kay made no bones about her own dislike of the woman. I sighed. If despising Brianna Bellamy was a reason for murder, it seemed half the inhabitants of Gray's Island could be suspects.

Uppermost in my mind was my reluctant decision to find the killer of the former pop star. Disliking the woman was too broad of a category which meant I needed to narrow the field and to do that, I'd need to think about more than just motive. I was lost in thoughts about the best way to find my suspects when Bill cleared his throat.

A glance showed he was expecting a reply to a question I hadn't heard. "Sorry Bill, my mind was wandering."

He rose, pushing his chair toward the table. "S'okay, I was just wondering how those of us that love Madison could help." He nodded his head toward the road. "Several of the business association members have already contacted me about it; just thought you might have a suggestion."

"Oh! That's nice of y'all. I paid the retainer for an attorney right after they pulled her in, and he is going to try and get her released. But, if they charge her, he'll go for bail. I was going to—"

"Leave the bail to me and the association. We're all happy to help." He frowned. "But this attorney you found, is he any good? We gotta get Maddie off the hook."

"It's Max Bernard and he was the man I used to get Dewey out of trouble when Brannon arrested him for Megan Hearn's murder."

Bill's chubby face was wreathed in smiles. "Perfect! Though, way I hear it, you're the one that really saved your brother. Hey, you found that killer, why don't you do it again?"

"Well, as it happens, I thought I might snoop a bit; see if I can shine some light in another direction."

He grinned and patted my shoulder. "Excellent!" He ambled toward the kitchen. "With you on the case Madison has nothing to fear!"

Chapter Eight

Bill's confidence in my sleuthing abilities, while flattering, only added to the pressure I was feeling. To make matters worse, not long after leaving the Split Bean I got a call from Max Bernard letting me know that Maddie would be released within the hour.

It was great news, but the detention by police had caused another problem; Madison's landlady had requested she vacate immediately so now she was homeless. After a quick call to

Mama requesting she air out the guest room, The Colonel and I rushed over to the sheriff's department.

"Oh Holly, thank you! Mr. Bernard said you hired him and now you're letting me stay with you. I don't know how I can ever repay you."

"Nothing to repay, Maddie. We are all happy to help." We loaded the rest of her things into the Scout and headed for home.

Madison sighed and settled The Colonel onto her lap, since he refused to budge from *his* seat. "I can't believe Mrs. Wiley asked me to leave! I've been living with her since Daddy kicked me out."

Mrs. Wiley ran a boarding house to supplement her retirement. Since her home wasn't set up for apartments, she was choosy about who she rented rooms to. "Well, she's old and doesn't understand how the legal system works." I turned onto Bay Street and slowed for a school bus. "Don't judge her too harshly, Madison."

Madison huffed. "I'll try not to, but do you know she actually told me the reason I had to leave was because she didn't want to be murdered in her bed!"

"I'm so sorry this is happening to you, Madison." I shifted gears and then reached over, patting her hand in sympathy. "But not everyone feels that way. Why, Bill Graves and the Downtown Merchants Association have offered to help and will post your bail."

A gasp from my passenger made me wince. *Nice one, Holly!* "Not that you'll need it! They won't charge you so don't fret. Press that remote, will ya?"

She snorted and did as I'd requested. "How can you be so sure? That detective said—"

"That detective is a blowhard, looking for advancement above all else," I guided the truck through the gates that blocked our drive and drove on to the back of the house. Putting The Colonel on the ground, I dropped the tailgate so we could unload Madison's belongings.

"Don't pay Brannon any attention. Max is on top of the legal side of things, and I'm going to try and figure out who really committed this murder."

Her expression softened and tears welled in her eyes. "Thank you." She swiped at her eyes. "If anyone can figure this out, it's you."

Oh boy. The love and trust shining from her eyes made my stomach roll. I'd made promises, now it was time to back them up and I didn't have a clue where to start.

RACHEL LYNNE

With Madison firmly under Mama's wing, The Colonel and I made some excuses and took ourselves off to my office next to Glitter and Garlands. I'd been staring into space, racking my brain for a place to start investigating, when Connie walked through the door.

"Got it solved yet?"

"Pfff, I wish." I shoved the piece of blank paper across the desk. "Making real progress, don't ya think?"

Connie snorted and sat in the chair opposite mine. She glanced down at the desk. "What's the hold up?"

"Too many suspects, no evidence pointing to anyone, except Madison." I shrugged. "Shall I go on?"

She laughed. "Nah, I get the picture." She propped her chin in her hand and joined me in staring at the blank, white paper.

CAROLERS AND CORPSES

We sat that way for several minutes, until Connie blew out a breath and picked up an ink pen. "Okay, this is ridiculous. Let's go with what we know."

"And that is?" She frowned at me. "All right, all right, let me think. We know the probable time of death."

"Great!" Connie wrote a Roman numeral one and the words, *Time of Death*. "What time was determined?"

"Um, Tate said between a quarter after midnight and 1:00 a.m."

"All right, now who was at the park during those hours?"

I cast my mind back to who I'd seen when The Colonel and I found Dewey. "Dewey of course, Kay Emory, and Gary Walston." I watched as Connie drew three lines; one across the paper and two down the page, creating three columns. At the top, she wrote *Suspects, Reason in Park, and Motive*. "Who else?"

"Well, the DeMarco twins and Felicity Simms." Connie added the names and then looked back at me. "Put Brianna Bellamy Ross and Madison Ross on there." I visualized the crowd that had surrounded Dewey. "There was a man I didn't recognize and ..."

I chewed on my lower lip and swallowed past the lump in my throat. My reluctance to play detective was already high but knowing I'd have to speak with the other man I'd seen made my stomach roll.

"And? Was there someone else there?"

I nodded. "Yeah, Roland Dupree." His name came out as a whisper.

Connie's eyes widened and, after a long pause, she placed her hand over mine and squeezed. "You okay?"

"No, not even a little bit, but it can't be helped." I shook off my unease and nodded toward the list she'd made. "So those are all of the people that I know were in the park around the time that Brianna Bellamy was murdered— oh!" Connie looked up and quirked a brow. "Um, there was also a man sitting in his car when I pulled into the lot."

Connie nodded and scribbled on the paper.

Connie pushed the paper toward me and stood. "I have to get back to the store, you got this!"

She was out the door before I could respond that I wasn't sure *what* I had. With a sigh, I turned my attention to the list she'd helped me make. The first thing I needed to do was write down why everyone was at the scene.

Dewey was easy; he'd been there to patrol and keep watch over the holiday market. Kay, Gary, Felicity, and Brianna were members of the Gray's Island Community Choir and I'd given them permission to rehearse. That left me wondering why Madison, the DeMarcos, and Roland Dupree were present.

I also needed to know who the snazzy dresser was. At the time, I'd been too busy to pay much attention to him, but looking back, I realized he'd stood apart from the others and remained silent while they complained about being kept in the park.

The way he was dressed also gave me pause. White slacks, an oxford shirt, and a sport coat. While not typically casual attire for men in the Lowcountry, it wasn't unheard of; a coat in bright blue with green palm leaves however made him stick out like a sore thumb.

Making a note to find out who the uncommonly dressed man was, I moved on to Madison. With Brianna Bellamy leading the choir, I couldn't imagine Madison choosing to participate, so what had brought her back to the park that late?

The presence of the DeMarco siblings also gave me pause. From Vincente DeMarco's angry comments, I had gathered he was part of the choir, but I'd need to find out if his sister was a member. I also needed to know who the man sitting in his car was.

Satisfied I'd finally made a start at cracking the case, I tucked the list into my bag and attempted to rouse The Colonel. He was snug in the plush bed Connie had bought and I needed dynamite, or lacking the explosives, a couple of treats in order to get him moving.

We were crossing the parking lot of Cannery Wharf when my phone rang. "Hey Mama, I'm on my way— "

"Oh Holly Marie, come home!"

My mother's panicked tone set my heart racing. "Why? What's wrong? Is someone hurt?"

I juggled with the phone and The Colonel's leash while attempting to unlock the truck and make sense of Mama's frantic explanation.

"They're trying to climb the fence!"

Mama's voice ended with a sob. I boosted The Colonel into his seat and slammed the door. I set the phone on speaker and shouted over the rumble of the engine. "Who is trying to get into the yard?"

My mother continued rambling hysterically, making most of what she was saying unintelligible. In the background I could hear shouting and then, above the din rose the sound of breaking glass, followed by a raucous cheer.

CAROLERS AND CORPSES

"Mama! Hang up and call 911!" I slammed the truck into third and drove home like a mad woman.

Chapter Nine

Sweeping the last of a broken beer bottle into the dustpan, I dumped it into a cardboard box and put everything into the trash can before joining the police at the end of the driveway. My best friend and former boss, Craig Everette, gave some final instructions to the officers and then came over to me.

"Ms. Effie all right?"

"Yeah, I sent her to bed with a sleeping pill."

Craig nodded. "And Madison?"

CAROLERS AND CORPSES

"She's inside, huddled on the couch with The Colonel." I shook my head. "Poor kid is scared to death and blaming herself for this mess."

Craig sighed. "Those people are insane." He looked around, taking in the busted mailbox and driveway gate hanging by one hinge. "Things like this don't happen in Sanctuary Bay!"

"They do when a famous celebrity is murdered here." I snorted. "They were protesting their idol's murderer being released; at least that's what I gathered from the signs they carried and their shouts of 'Justice for Brianna.'"

Craig scowled and bent to pick up a broken sign. "Well, the lunatics are spending the night in jail, though the courts won't hold them longer than that." I tagged along as he walked to the trash can. "Gonna have to do something before they're released, Holly."

My shoulders drooped. He wasn't saying anything I hadn't already figured out, but hearing it said aloud pressed the point. I let out a ragged breath. "Not sure what, though."

"Well, for starters, get Madison out of here."

"But Craig, she has nowhere else to go! I can't just kick her to the curb."

He nodded toward the broken gates. "It'll be a few days before you can get those repaired. All the protestors will have trespassing added to the list of charges if they come back but ..." He shook his head and sighed. "From what I saw tonight, I doubt that will be much of a deterrent. Ms. Effie, and Madison for that matter, won't be safe here."

Mulling over the truth bombs he'd dropped, I searched for a solution. "I guess she could go to a hotel ... no!"

"What? Got an idea? Because you're just going to create madness for more people if she goes to a hotel."

"Got a better idea. She can stay at Myrtlewood."

Craig's eyebrows rose. "Not a bad idea, but it's pretty isolated out there on Saint Mariana Island."

Myrtlewood Plantation sat on forty acres, with only two ways in—via the gated drive or by boat. The estate had been in Mama's family for over a century and was rarely used aside from holiday celebrations and family get-togethers. While equipped with electricity and running water, there was no cable or internet, and cell service was iffy at best.

"Under the circumstances, that isn't a bad thing. The trick will be getting Madison out there without anyone being the wiser."

CAROLERS AND CORPSES

Before dawn the next morning, The Colonel and I left the house with Madison tucked into the backseat, hidden by a blanket. Once I'd assured myself we weren't being followed, I took Madison to the grocery store and, loaded down with provisions, we set off for Saint Mariana Island.

We were unloading the groceries when it occurred to me that Madison could do me a favor while she hid from the crazy fans of Brianna Bellamy.

"Maddie, we'll be hosting Christmas here and I haven't gotten around to putting up any decorations." I folded the last of the paper bags and stored them in a cupboard. "Interested in killing time by making the place festive?"

Madison grinned. "Oh, I'd love to!"

"Awesome! Come on, the decorations are in the attic."

Several trips down the stairs later, the front parlor was overflowing with plastic bins. Madison put a Christmas playlist on her phone and happily dove in, removing the various decorations and sorting them into piles.

Whistling for The Colonel, I left Madison to her fun and wandered outside to make sure the grounds were secure. Nestled among ancient live oaks, the main house wasn't visible from the road. We rented the fields out to a local farmer though, and he'd cut a dirt road from his property to the equipment shed that sat on the western property line.

When we'd arrived, I'd noticed Jed Prine was repairing fences along our boundary, so I set off across the barren field. I wanted to let him know someone was staying at the house and ask him to keep an eye on things since she'd be alone.

The Colonel rushed ahead, darting in and out of the tall grass bordering the field as he followed the scent of something his pudgy butt couldn't hope to catch.

My leg's unpredictability and the need for a cane meant taking my time on the rutted dirt, but I was in no hurry. It'd been weeks since my schedule had allowed me to stop and smell the roses and I wasn't going to waste any opportunity that came my way.

CAROLERS AND CORPSES

The weather was typical for December—warm and sunny, though the brilliant blue sky was rapidly filling with gray tinted clouds. A cold front was predicted for later in the week, and we'd likely see frost by Christmas. Still, I'd enjoy the warmth while it lasted.

The live oaks creaked as a strong gust blew in off the river. I threw my head back and reveled in the sharp, slightly rotten tang of decaying cord grass and crustaceans that drifted on the breeze as the tide went out. Living in the Lowcountry was always a joy but I relished the fall and winter months when the lower heat and humidity and absence of bugs made it a paradise.

The patch of fence Jed was mending stood several hundred yards away and my progress slowed as my leg began to protest. I was regretting my decision not to take the UTV when The Colonel managed to flush a rabbit. His frantic barking caught Jed's attention and he met me halfway.

"Mornin' Holly, haven't seen you since Thanksgiving."

"Hey Jed, busy time of year." I nodded toward the section of fence he'd been mending. "Big job? I can get Dewey to come out and give you a hand."

"Nah, thanks anyway." Jed wiped his face with a bandana. "Limb fell when that storm blew through the other night. Figured I'd better get it mended before I turn 'ol Seamus loose."

The last bit of apprehension I had about leaving Madison alone at Myrtlewood vanished. There'd been a small possibility of someone gaining access to the property via Jed's property, but no one was going to cross the field with a 1500-pound Texas Longhorn bull roaming free.

Grinning like a fool, I filled Jed in on the situation with Madison. With his assurances he'd both keep her presence a secret and watch out for her, The Colonel and I made our way back.

Arriving at the house, I found a wreath hung on the front door and a beautiful gold and white topiary holding pride of place on the foyer table, but a cursory glance into the parlor revealed it was still a mess of holiday decorations. The room was also bereft of humans.

Using the sound of carols as a homing beacon, I found Madison perched on a step stool attempting to hang a wreath on the gilt mirror above the buffet. My arrival startled her and she overbalanced. I hobbled over and managed to steady the ladder, saving her from a nasty fall.

CAROLERS AND CORPSES

"Having second thoughts about leaving you alone to decorate!"

Maddie laughed. "Ah, it could happen to anyone." She finished with the wreath and made a production of hopping off the stool. "See? Perfectly safe."

I snorted and started rummaging in the boxes. "Got a plan for this room? We usually set a buffet up in here on Christmas Eve, so it'll see lots of traffic."

Madison's smile was hesitant. "Well, I was thinking of a simple coastal theme? If that's okay, I mean this room has the marble fireplace and the wide molding and the furniture is so pretty..." She shrugged. "Be a shame to overpower it all."

"I agree! Carry on."

She grinned and started gathering supplies from a box sitting on the table before carrying it all to the fireplace.

Content to let her run with it and curious about what she'd create, I stood to the side and watched as Madison placed a strip of battery-operated lights on top of the marble slab and then wove a length a tulle around them.

Once the wispy fabric was placed to her satisfaction, she gathered a finely woven net into scallops tied with a length of knotted hemp rope. Scattered amongst the fabric and netting were clusters of shells, a starfish, and a few nautical navigational instruments. The effect was stunning.

"I love it! Very elegant and totally coastal. Great job!"

Her smile was brief. She turned back to her mantle arrangement and frowned. "Thanks, but it needs something." She dug through the boxes and then sighed. "The shells are cream and pink, and the other items are in tones of brown and tan. I need some blues and greens, don't you think?"

Considering her design, I agreed. The gray and white marble blended with her chosen items. "At Connie's shop there are some stems of aqua colored coral branches that might look good sticking out above the tulle."

"Oh, that would be perfect!" She glanced up at the wreath she'd hung in front of the buffet mirror. "What about adding some lamb's ear leaves and maybe some eucalyptus?"

I nodded. "Great idea. I'll grab some while I'm at the office." I looked at the boxes of decorations waiting to be unpacked. Most of the items had been in the family for generations.

Mama's nativity set always held pride of place on the buffet, a grouping of ceramic Christmas houses were displayed in the library, and a train that had been my father's belonged beneath the main Christmas tree that would stand in the parlor. The rest of the boxes contained swags and stems of evergreens, magnolia leaves, boxwood, and dozens of tree ornaments in too many color palettes to count.

"Okay, I'll make sure those things are in their usual places; family traditions are important to me." Her smile dimmed. "Especially since all of mine have been ruined."

Several expressions of sympathy crossed my mind but, in the end, they were just platitudes. Madison's only living relative was gone and all of her family possessions were out of reach, for the near future anyway. Deciding to lift the mood, I kept my reply light.

"Well, if we're holding to tradition, we should be singing carols while we decorate."

As I'd hoped, Madison laughed. "Oh no, you don't want me to join in that custom. According to my music teacher, I'm hopelessly tone deaf!"

We laughed and began assembling the flocked artificial tree that always resided in front of the picture window opposite the fireplace. We inserted the final branch when Madison's inability to sing popped into my mind.

Sweeping the shed needles into a pile, I casually asked, "Madison, you said you can't sing?"

She looked up from stringing the lights around the tree and nodded. "Honest. You don't want to hear me belt out a song!"

I laughed. "I'll take your word for it." I bit my lip and chose my words carefully. "Why were you in the park Sunday night then? If you weren't there for choir practice."

As I'd intended, she seemed to place no special importance on my question, merely shrugging as she continued decorating the tree. "I thought I'd left my sewing bag in the craft tent."

Weighing her reply against the events of that night, I frowned. "So, you went looking for it after midnight?" I couldn't hide the skepticism in my voice.

Wide eyed, Madison set down a package of glass ornaments and joined me by the buffet. Tears welled in her eyes and her bottom lip quivered. "Are you doubting my innocence, Holly?"

Shaking my head, I patted her hand. "No, definitely not! However, it does seem a bit odd that you'd go back to the craft booth that late."

Madison bit her lip. "I guess I hadn't thought about how it looks, now that she's dead." She fiddled with a chenille stem. "After our argument, I went home like you'd told me. I ... I cried myself to sleep and woke up a little after eleven. I couldn't go back to sleep and thought I'd finish the little coat you asked me to make for The Colonel." She shrugged. "That's all, really. I just wanted something to do, you know, to take my mind off things."

With a nod, I started unpacking Mama's nativity as I considered what Maddie had told me. Lost in thought, I jumped when she cleared her throat.

"I shouldn't have been there!" She sniffed and scrubbed at her tear-filled eyes. "They're going to throw me into prison!"

"Maddie ..." I gave her a quick hug and then guided her back toward the tree. "It does look bad, but we'll figure out who really killed Brianna. Just ... you need to stay positive and keep busy."

She blew her nose and gave me a wobbly smile before resuming her task. Once I finished the buffet decorations, I went into the kitchen and fixed lunch.

"Grilled cheese and tomato soup, Maddie."

She finished running garland around the tree and joined me at the table. We chatted about decorations and Christmas Eve menu ideas and then I broached the elephant in the room.

Stacking our empty dishes on the tray, I considered the questions left after Connie helped me make the list of suspects. "Maddie, what time did you enter the park?"

She looked up from her phone. "Uh, not sure, maybe midnight? A little after ... wait!" Muttering under her breath, she fiddled with her phone. "Where did I save that ... ah perfect!" She looked up and grinned. "Twenty-two minutes after twelve."

My brows rose. "That's awfully specific."

"Yep, because I made a note to contact the parks and rec people."

"What about?"

"How dark it was at the side of the park. I was going to enter through the small lot close to the bonfire area, cuz I have a gate key, but most of the lights were off at that end. So I drove around to the main parking area."

I frowned. Goodwin Park was always well lit, but we'd added extra lights via the poles Gary Walston's crew installed. The market lights should have been burning. I thought back to when Dewey and I were walking over to Santa's Workshop; we'd been able to see well enough, though I had needed my flashlight once I passed the craft tents. What had happened to those lights?

I made a mental note to see if the lights were broken or if it was possible someone had tampered with them. According to Maddie's notes, she'd been near the murder scene at 12:22

CAROLERS AND CORPSES

a.m. and the estimated time of Brianna Bellamy's death was determined to be between 12:15 a.m. and 1:00 a.m.

Bellamy could have been under that snow drift when Maddie attempted to retrieve her sewing bag. I broached the possibility.

Madison's eyes widened. "Gosh, I hadn't thought of that! To think, if I hadn't been so busy looking for my bag, she might have been saved."

I quickly disabused her of the notion. "Don't beat yourself up, Maddie. According to Tate, she was unconscious before someone put the snow powder in her mouth. He suspects she was drugged or maybe poisoned." I shrugged. "It's doubtful finding her at that point would have saved her."

Madison gulped. "Poisoned? Oh my, that's horrible! I didn't like her, but dying like that." She shuddered. "I wouldn't wish that on anyone."

"No, me either. But, if she was already dead or dying when you got your bag raises the possibility that the killer was still in the area. Did you happen to hear or see anything unusual?"

Color fading from her face, Maddie wrapped her arms around herself. "I don't think so, but wow, how scary that I could have run into the person that did this." She started to rise from her chair when her eyes widened, and her mouth dropped open. She sank back down and met my gaze. "I just remembered something. There was this weird noise."

I frowned. "Weird how? Where was it coming from?"

"Um, I had just walked out of the sewing tent. I was looking around the other tents when—"

"Wait, why were you in the other craft booths?"

"My sewing bag wasn't where I thought I'd left it." She shrugged. "I wasn't really looking in the other tents, just walking around kinda looking to see if somehow it'd been moved or, I don't know, I was confused because I am still pretty sure I left that bag under the table."

"They found your scissors near the body and The Colonel found his coat not far from there. Someone is trying to frame you, I think."

"What? Why? What have I done to deserve that?"

I sighed. "Nothing Madison, you just made a convenient target." I shook off my growing anger and tried to focus on finding a killer. A young woman had lost her life, and another was in danger of having her life ruined. Someone needed to pay.

"Don't try and understand the motivations of a person willing to kill, Madison. It'll drive you mad. Tell me more about the noise you heard. Why was it weird?"

CAROLERS AND CORPSES

She bit her lip and stared at a point behind me. "Well, it was a whirling sound. I remember thinking someone was driving a golf cart."

My brow furrowed as I considered what she'd said. A golf cart? They were common in the gated golf communities, and we had one for use on the plantation. It was easier for Mama to drive than the UTV. But I couldn't recall seeing anyone in town operate such a thing. In fact, they weren't street legal in Sanctuary Bay.

The puzzle of what Madison had heard was pushed to the back of my mind in favor of more pressing questions. Namely, who were the two men I hadn't recognized. I asked Maddie and got a shrug for my troubles.

"Sorry Holly, I didn't see anyone in their car when I drove up. I noticed the guy in the funny looking jacket though. He didn't look like a local."

"My thoughts exactly. It was a wild coat!" I pushed away from the table and picked up the tray of dirty dishes. "I'll straighten up the kitchen and then I need to be off. Is there anything besides the floral picks from Glitter and Garland that you need?"

Madison shook her head. "Not that I can think of except, do you have another tree for the parlor? I'm gonna start decorating that room when I finish in here."

"One of those boxes we brought down should have another full-sized artificial tree. We put that one in the sunroom; there are coastal themed ornaments that go with it. But feel free to shake things up and do something different." I snorted. "Lord knows we have every color and theme imaginable since Mama likes to shop after Christmas sales! Unless you want to do something different, we usually get a live tree for the parlor."

"That sounds nice. I'm not looking to change your traditions."

I smiled and started for the kitchen. "Okay, then I'll have Dewey bring one out as soon as he can."

The washing up only took a few minutes. I dried the last dish and looked around. Satisfied that everything was shipshape, I called The Colonel and headed to the truck; time to get down to business and catch a killer.

Chapter Ten

My plan had been to drop Madison off at Myrtlewood and then go into my office but, after learning some of the lights had been out in the area where the murder had taken place, I decided to swing by the park and take a look.

The holiday market was hopping, with people milling about in the vendor stalls, kids lined up for a visit with Santa, and families enjoying the activities in Reindeer Games and crafts in Santa's Workshop.

The Colonel was wiggling with excitement, people equaled potential cuddles or food to him, and he was eager to explore. But I was on a mission. I avoided the crowds by taking the path that ran closest to the river.

Keeping The Colonel to a firm pace, we reached the end of the boardwalk and cut across the park, skirting the crowds by picking our way through the maze of tent guide wires and electric cords that covered the grass behind the attractions.

Madison had said the lights closest to her group's craft tent had been out. We were in sight of the temporary pole for that section when I saw a man prop a ladder against the pole and climb.

Vaguely recognizing him as one of Gary Walston's crew, I approached and called out. "Whatcha doin' up there?"

The man looked down and waved. "Hey Ms. Daye! Just a second." He stretched an arm's length and touched all the bulbs, working his way back to the pole before descending the ladder.

"Hi, you work for Gary Walston, right?"

He nodded. "Yes ma'am, Bob Fender. I helped put the poles up last week."

CAROLERS AND CORPSES

"Thanks again, y'all were life savers. But how did you know something was wrong with these lights? I was just coming to inspect them after someone complained."

He grinned. "I beat ya to it! The family and I were walking around the market when a friend who has that vendor booth over there mentioned this string of lights keeps flickering. Figured I'd check it out."

"I appreciate it." I glanced up. "Did you figure out what's wrong?"

He dragged a hand through his hair and sighed. "Nothing wrong with the main switch so I'm trying all of the bulbs, figure one of them is loose."

"Oh, would that make them go out?"

He nodded and moved the ladder farther down the line of lights. "Yeah, these things are like Christmas lights. If one goes out, all the ones on that strand will go. Hold on a sec, gonna check these middle ones." He climbed up and repeated his process of checking all the bulbs within reach. Finding nothing amiss, he moved the ladder toward the other pole and started again.

The Colonel was snorting around on the ground when he suddenly tugged on his leash. I was following along making sure he didn't shake the ladder as he inspected every inch of ground beneath the light pole when something red caught my eye.

I'd just picked it up when the electrician came up beside me.

"That was the problem."

"What was wrong?" The glossy red paper seemed to be part of a candy wrapper. Leave it to The Colonel to find potential food! I shoved the paper into my pocket until I could find a trash can and turned my attention to Bob.

"That bulb at the far end was loose." He snorted. "Figures it would be at the opposite end of where I started. I tightened it so they should be fine now."

"Thanks so much! I really appreciate y'all taking time away from work to do this."

He shrugged. "No problem, we been out of work for a few weeks now. Sure hope that causeway job comes through, or it'll be a lean Christmas."

"You guys are out of work?"

Bob nodded. "Yeah, boss kept a few of us on payroll doing odd jobs but if we don't get that causeway …" He turned and started folding up the ladder. "He's playin' it close to the vest, but I been with him for over ten years, he's not foolin' me." He shook his head and tucked the ladder under his arm. "He

CAROLERS AND CORPSES

bet the lot building spec houses and then the market tanked. Gonna put this back and track down my family. You have a nice afternoon, Ms. Daye and, well, fingers crossed the causeway job goes through."

"Yes, absolutely wishing y'all the best and thanks again for taking care of the lights." Bob strolled away, leaving me and The Colonel to make our way back to the parking lot. My mind was turning over what he'd said.

I hadn't had any idea Gary's business was in dire straits and guilt was rising in me; I needed to see about getting him a check for all the work his company did. He shouldn't have to take a financial hit simply because the public works department couldn't get their act together.

The Colonel and I were almost at the main gates when we walked past a trashcan and I remembered the paper I'd shoved into my pocket. Coaxing The Colonel to a halt, I dug into my pocket and pulled out the red piece of paper.

Hand hovering over the can, I was about to let it fall when my gaze landed on the white lettering. L O V E. A Valentine message? Too early. But something was familiar about the shape of the paper and the color.

Raising it for a better look, the pungent scent of spices I associated with the holidays reached my nose and my brain kicked into gear adding two and two: The red paper was a gum wrapper.

Specifically, a Clove gum wrapper. A vivid memory of Gary Walston chomping gum Sunday night rose in my mind. Already a suspect on my list, the gum wrapper, combined with his familiarity with the market lights moved him to the top of my list.

Lost in thoughts of what reason Gary Walston might have had to kill Brianna Bellamy, I almost ignored the man in the flashy blue jacket walking down Bay Street.

I slowed and watched from the rearview mirror as he, along with a little fawn colored French bulldog, entered Meows and Growls pet store. Making a split-second decision, I found a parking spot and followed him into the store.

CAROLERS AND CORPSES

The Colonel was well known and so well loved in the pet store that the owner, Stanley Thigpen, had created a special dog biscuit named for him. As usual, he trotted up to the counter as if he owned the place and stared at the attendant until she handed over his treat.

I'd been mentally running through possible conversation starters that wouldn't make me look like a nut, but the Frenchie saw treats were on offer and in no time he and The Colonel were fast friends.

"Hey guys, no rough housing in the store." The dogs ignored me, of course.

"Clyde! That's where you got to." The man I'd seen at the park strolled up from the back of the store carrying a couple of cans of dog food. He placed them on the counter and grinned. "Sorry about that, he's an escape artist."

"He's no trouble and his energy is rubbing off on The Colonel; little piglet needs some exercise." We both chuckled. I debated beating around the bush but, as Mama could attest, I didn't have a subtle bone in my body.

"Um, didn't I see you the other night in the park with the carolers?

"Uh, yeah. I was there." His smile faded and his gaze jumped around from me to the dogs. He paid for his purchase. "Okay buddy, time to put the leash back on." It took a few minutes to wrestle the little French bulldog back into his harness. Once he'd secured the dog he glanced at me. "We should meet up at the dog park sometime, Clyde is lonely."

"How about now? If you have time, that is. I wanted to talk to you anyway."

He frowned and moved toward the door. "What about?"

I laid my cards on the table. "I'm Holly Daye. I retired from the sheriff's department and now I decorate for events. The young girl accused of killing Brianna Bellamy works for me and I'm not convinced the detective assigned to the case is diligently gathering all the facts."

"So, you're helping out."

Opening the door, I guided The Colonel through and waited to answer until we were out on the sidewalk; I hadn't missed the cashier's avid expression and had no desire to add fuel to the fire of gossip so common in Sanctuary Bay. "Unofficially, yes. I'm trying to get a feel for what happened that night."

He nodded. "Sure, okay. Let's grab a cup of coffee and we can talk while the dogs play."

CAROLERS AND CORPSES

Conversation in the Split Bean changed to whispers a few minutes after we entered, with even the baristas giving us strange looks. Once we had our orders and were back outside, I apologized. "Sorry about that, we're a tourist town. You'd think people would be used to strangers."

He choked on his coffee. "It's all right, I'm used to it and much more actually."

"What do you mean?"

He laughed. "Gotta hand it to this place, makes a guy humble."

At my puzzled frown he laughed again.

"Don't you recognize me?"

"No, sorry, should I?"

He shook his head. "Not really. I'm Justin Gambrell."

My expression must have shown my confusion because he snorted and clued me in. "The Sweet Life?"

I shook my head and shrugged causing him to laugh again. "It's the tagline for the soda commercials I was in ... forget it, what was it you wanted to talk to me about?"

From what he'd said, I assumed he was famous but, as with the fame of Brianna Bellamy, I had no clue what he was known for and didn't really care; I had a killer to find.

"If you aren't from Gray's Island, what were you doing at the community's choir practice?"

He smirked. "I am or was friends with Brianna. We were on the *Tomorrow's Pop Star* show. I was at loose ends after my commercial contract ended and she invited me out. She said it was to keep her company, but right before I got on the plane she texted me, requesting I sing with her choir. I was brought in to do the solo parts."

My brows rose. "Bet that made some people mad."

Justin chuckled. "Oh yeah, that pompous guy Vincente was pretty ticked off when she introduced me."

So that was what Vincente DeMarco was at the park for; I hadn't known he sang with the choir, much less that he was their star. I wondered if his sister, Valentina, was also a singer.

"Huh-uh, she played the piano for them. Gotta say, she's not bad."

Huh, Valentina was also a decent artist from what I'd seen of her face painting. Artistic talent must run in the DeMarco genes. "I got to the park after one and was pretty surprised to find y'all still there. When Gary asked permission for the choir to stay and rehearse I'd assumed it would only be for an hour or so."

CAROLERS AND CORPSES

He snorted. "Should have been but Brianna, as usual, was late. We didn't get started until almost midnight." He rolled his eyes. "Then all of the drama happened ... total waste of time."

"Drama?"

"Oh yeah, seemed like the whole choir had a beef with her!"

I frowned. "What happened to make you say that?"

He laughed. "Better question is what *didn't* happen!" He tipped his head back and drained the paper cup, then rose to toss it in the metal can before continuing. "I guess it all kicked off when Brianna kept everyone waiting for over an hour. Gotta say I was angry too, but that older lady with the short red hair ..."—he met my gaze and frowned—"Felicity maybe?"

I nodded. "Felicity Simms. I think she was the former choir director."

"Yeah, that's her. Boy she was ticked! She started in on Brianna about a bunch of stuff, something about a flower? I don't know, her rant was all over the place but some of it was about how unprofessional Brianna was for keeping us all waiting. Oh, and that Brianna was too big for her britches? I was about rolling on the ground at that one!"

My eyes widened. "And what did Brianna have to say about that?"

Justin smirked. "Well, you know Brianna— er, you probably don't but, she had this way about her. She liked to push people's buttons. When the old lady paused for breath, Brianna rolled her eyes and said that Felicity was just mad because they'd made her choir director and walked toward the stage. Then, typical Bri, she turns back and smirks at Felicity and says, 'Are you still mad that your husband was sniffing around trying to pick me up?'" Justin huffed. "Then, to pile more crap on the fire, Brianna makes this innocent face and says, 'Oh, you *are*! Is that why you made Eugene sit in the car?'"

Woah, that would have set any woman off. Brianna Bellamy had gone after older men, especially those with money. Felicity Simms was angry with Brianna over flirting with her husband; now I knew who I'd seen sitting in his car that night.

"I didn't know Brianna Bellamy but from what you're telling me, seems as if she loved goading people."

"You could say that." The bulldogs tired of their games and came back to us. After making room on the bench for both dogs, Justin continued. "Leave it to Brianna to make it all worse. She flirted with married men in Hollywood, too. It's why she left. Anyway, Felicity stormed off in tears and then Bri thought we'd all just carry on like nothing had happened!"

"Wow, that's ..." I shook my head at the antics of the victim; I wouldn't go so far as to say she deserved what happened to her but if ever someone was asking for it ... "If y'all didn't rehearse without Felicity why didn't everyone leave?"

Justin sighed. "Me and another guy were ready to pack it in, but the others started in on Brianna for upsetting Felicity, so Bri shouted at everyone and then told them to take a break. She took off across the park and that's the last any of us saw of her."

Frowning, I replayed what Justin had said. "What time was this? When she called for a break?"

His eyebrows rose and he looked off at the river as he considered my question. "Um, I remember looking at my phone when Brianna showed up and it was about a quarter after eleven, then she got into it with Felicity so ... we must have taken a break near midnight or shortly after?"

Filing that information, I nodded. "Close to midnight and the coroner puts her time of death between a quarter after midnight and one. What did everyone do when Brianna left?"

Justin shrugged. "I'm not sure. Valentina looked fit to be tied. She jumped up from the piano so fast she knocked her stool over. I picked it up but didn't see where she went. The others were standing around bickering when I bugged out."

I considered everything Justin had said. While Gary Walston was still at the top of my list, Felicity Simms had risen to the second spot, though her husband could probably be ruled out. I'd need to know where everyone else was, starting with Justin.

"You left during the break? Where did you go?"

Justin stiffened and his eyes narrowed. "Am I a suspect?"

There was no sense in lying. "Technically, but only because you were present. It doesn't sound like you had a beef with Brianna."

His shoulders relaxed and a rueful smile graced his face. "No, we were friends, if anyone in the Hollywood rat race can be friends. Still, when everyone took a break, I went to the gas station down the street. I'd just flown in and was running on fumes since Brianna stood me up for dinner. I grabbed an energy drink and a protein bar. I've probably got the receipt somewhere."

"Thanks, but I can get Pug Ziggler's security cameras if it comes to that."

A murmur of voices brought both dogs awake. They jumped down and started barking as two men with cameras hanging from their necks came into view.

Justin swore and rose. "Paparazzi!" He scooped Clyde up and waved. "Gotta run, nice meeting you Holly."

CAROLERS AND CORPSES

He took off before I could reply. Deprived of their prey, the reporters started sizing me up; probably trying to decide if I was anyone famous. Snapping The Colonel's lead to his collar, I hurried off before they got any closer. I had no desire to make it into tomorrow's paper; the shooting had given me enough notoriety to last a lifetime.

Chapter Eleven

Brackish water was lapping at the sides of the causeway as I crossed over to Gray's Island the following afternoon, making me anxious; I'd need to cut my conversation short if I didn't want to be stuck on the island until the tide went out.

I'd awakened with a list of 'To Dos' and good intentions but Mama's list of *Holly Dos* was longer. It was closing in on four o'clock before I was able to set out for Felicity Simms's house.

CAROLERS AND CORPSES

Thankfully, the Simms house faced the marsh. Once across the causeway, it was a short jaunt down a live oak lined, sandy road.

After a wait that left me tapping my foot, Eugene opened the door. I'd come ready with an excuse for calling on Felicity, but Eugene merely shrugged and led me out the patio doors and down a brick path to a small greenhouse.

"Holly Daye's here to see you, Fliss. I'll put a pot of coffee and some Christmas cookies on the picnic table if you want."

"Holly! What a surprise." Felicity waved Eugene away. "That'll be nice dear, then you go on back to your model trains." She winked at me. "Boys and their toys."

I smiled and shortened The Colonel's leash as we stepped into the small, glass-sided room. Felicity's greenhouse was located on the far side of a tropical paradise. Brick paths meandered through a garden of lush foliage surrounding a koi pond. I recognized elephant ears and sago palms along with camellias, holly, and boxwood. There were also pots of mums, pansies, and snapdragons. The effect was stunning, and I could only imagine what an oasis her garden would be in the height of summer.

Motioning me to join her, Felicity continued with her work at the potting bench. Along one wall stood a low table covered with seedling flats, while the other spaces were home to an abundance of cold-sensitive plants I was hard pressed to name. The center of the greenhouse was reserved for orchids; a bewildering collection that I guessed, judging by the way she was fussing with them, were Felicity Simms's passion.

"What brings you out today?" Felicity sprayed something on one of the orchids and then picked up another and removed it from its pot.

My mind screamed get to the point so I could be on my way before the tide changed, but common sense overrode my anxiety. "Your gardens are lovely, and this greenhouse is amazing, I've never seen so many orchids!"

As I'd intended, Felicity was happy to tell me all about her hobby. What followed was an enthusiastic lecture on all things orchid which culminated in one fact useful to my quest for a killer; Brianna Bellamy had been the neighbor from hell and her pet goat had escaped the yard and eaten a prized orchid that Felicity had saved for three years to purchase. If that wasn't a strong reason for someone like Felicity to strike back, I didn't know what was.

Her rant on the horrors of living next to Brianna Bellamy wound down and I seized my chance to turn the conversation. "My word, you must have really despised the woman." I schooled my features into what I hoped was an expression of sympathy. "And after all you suffered, the council appointing her to choir director was like rubbing salt in the wound."

"Yes! You see? Normal people understand what I went through!" She finished potting an orchid and placed it on a nearby table. "That woman was an abomination. Why, it was bad enough she let that little goat get into my yard but the wild parties, loud music at all hours of the day and night, and let's not forget her prancing around naked for all the world to see. I complained to our HOA, but it did no good so then I called the police."

"Did that solve the issues?"

Felicity snorted. "No, because *we don't have a noise ordinance on the books.*" Her tone was mocking, leaving me no doubt she was quoting some nameless bureaucrat.

"That's a shame. Why didn't your homeowner's association step in?"

Felicity's expression darkened. "I have no idea, except that they are spineless! I wasn't the only one that complained you know, most people on this island couldn't stand her for one reason or another. You should have seen the way she acted once Clayton Ross married her."

My ears perked up. "What difference did it make that she was married to Mr. Ross?"

She huffed. "He was the chairman of the island council as well as being wealthy and having influence with many state politicians. She used his position to get her way." She rolled her eyes. "Campaign donations can buy a lot of power."

On that, Felicity and I agreed; I'd seen it too many times during the years I was married to Brooks. There was a reason his law partner was now our congressman. But how, I wondered, had Clayton Ross's political influence been used by Brianna?

Felicity was happy to inform me.

"Oh, she lorded it over us all." Felicity snorted. "Playing Lady Bountiful at every meeting."

Imagining how Mama and her friends would react to a young woman putting on airs, it wasn't hard to believe Brianna had caused resentment.

"Yes," Felicity agreed. "But that isn't what made her persona non-grata on the island." She tsked and shook her head. "No, that was because she persuaded Clayton to go back on his support for the causeway."

My brows rose. "What? Why would she do that?" The causeway was a big deal for those often trapped by the rising tides and unstable road.

Felicity pursed her lips. "She claimed it was over concerns for the marsh and wildlife, but she was overheard to say the new road would hinder her view and bring noise pollution." She met my gaze and then nodded toward her dock. "You know the proposal moves it within sight of our homes." She shrugged. "I can't say I like the idea of our peaceful cove being disturbed but the engineers felt it was the best place and there is no denying we need a new road!"

She'd get no disagreement from me, and I didn't even live on the island. Still, protesting the building of a road was surely not enough reason to kill a woman. To my surprise, Felicity was only lukewarm in her support of my statement.

"I'm sorry she's dead but the woman was asking for it. If the way she treated me and my property is any indication of her behavior toward others ..."

"But, Felicity, if she was such a pariah why would the council make her choir director?"

Felicity rolled her eyes. "J.T. Minton, that's why. He wants us to win the state competition this year because his company is a major sponsor. But we were fine without that little tramp." She huffed and started misting her orchids. "It is beyond me how she won that TV contest; she was a mediocre singer at best." Felicity glanced at me and quirked an eyebrow. "The girl had a limited range and liked to show off instead of blending her voice with the rest of us. I have no doubts that her leadership would have led to our loss at state."

Whether or not Brianna Bellamy was a decent singer or even capable of choir leadership, Felicity Simms had been deposed from the position and anything she had to say on the subject was going to look like sour grapes. I cleared my throat and decided to get down to the business upper most in my mind.

"Felicity, I've been talking to some people that were present at the park the night Brianna died." She glanced up from her work and frowned, but I ignored her and plowed ahead. "You had a heated argument with Brianna Bellamy."

Felicity took exception to my statement. "So? I just told you everyone hated her."

"Yes, but I'm questioning everyone, and multiple people said your argument was bad enough to send you running off in tears."

CAROLERS AND CORPSES

Eyes wide and face red, Felicity set the orchid she'd been holding back on the table with a thud. "Are you accusing me? How dare you? What gives you the right?"

My brows rose. "Would you rather I tell Detective Brannon and have him bring you in for questioning?"

She paled and her anger deflated as quickly as it had arisen. Felicity seemed unaware that Brannon was a clueless flunky only looking for promotion, and I was happy to keep her in the dark.

Felicity sighed and set the plant mister on to the potting bench. "What do you want to know?"

"Is it true she tried to seduce your husband?" Normally, I stayed clear of sordid gossip but now it appeared to be relevant.

Her face flushed and her blue eyes were shiny with unshed tears as she nodded. "Yes, but then she met Clayton and he had way more money and influence than Eugene, so she set her sights on him and left us in peace, well she stopped making advances anyway."

Jealousy was a powerful motivator, but did Felicity Simms have it in her to commit murder? Taken on its own, I might have paused, but Brianna Bellamy had caused the Simms nothing but trouble and her irresponsible pet ownership had led to the destruction of a much prized and expensive orchid. I couldn't rule her out. "Where were you at the time she called a break?"

Felicity's eyes narrowed. She glared at me for a minute but when I didn't back down, she huffed. "If you must know, I was walking along the river, trying to clear my head and calm down enough to finish rehearsals."

Her voice held a ring of truth, though her strolling the river walk didn't mean she hadn't strayed to the area behind Santa's Workshop. My own journey the other day had taken that route. "Can anyone verify that?"

She scowled. "Yes, as it happens, Valentina DeMarco joined me not long after I left."

Shoulders thrown back, chin jutted forward, and eyes hard, Felicity's tone had been aggressive and challenging. Something told me the offer of cookies and coffee was no longer on the table.

While only about a decade older than me, Felicity was active with the historical society and had worked with Mama on several projects. I would likely hear a lecture on badgering her friends.

CAROLERS AND CORPSES

This amateur detective role was a thankless task. I decided against further antagonism by keeping my intentions of checking her alibi to myself and simply nodded.

"Now, if that's all, I'd like you to leave."

Her shoulders relaxed, though her jaw was still clenched as I gathered the slack in The Colonel's leash and made my way back to the truck. Conscious of the unstable causeway, I was more than happy to leave Felicity Simms to her orchids.

Loading The Colonel into the truck, I hobbled around and hoisted myself into the driver's seat then paused for a breath. The rising tide and faulty road were uppermost in my mind, but my leg was protesting the idea of operating the clutch on the old truck.

I gritted my teeth against the throb in my thigh and put the Scout into gear; the sooner I got home and into the hot tub, the better. I'd also need to call my physical therapist and move my appointment up.

I'd just turned onto the main road when flashing police lights and slowing traffic let me know I wouldn't be soaking in steamy water anytime soon. With a sigh, I guided the gearshift into neutral and waited for the cars in front of me to drive up to the widened part of the road meant to be used as a turnaround when the causeway flooded.

It seemed to take ages for everyone to get themselves sorted. I drummed my fingers on the steering wheel and tried to ignore The Colonel's sighs and fidgeting. It was close to supper time, and I was about to be stranded on Gray's Island with a ticked off bulldog. Another couple of minutes and it was finally my turn. Once redirected, I cursed Gray's Island and their crappy road all the way to the other side of the island.

My stomach growled and The Colonel kept looking at my upholstery like it'd be the worse for wear if his belly wasn't filled immediately, so I decided to make the best of a bad situation and have dinner at the Laurel Creek Marina. I set the emergency brake and limped around to get my wiggling ball of pudge.

"Come on, buddy, dinner is on me."

The restaurant wasn't crowded, but I elected to sit on the patio since The Colonel would be scarfing food with his usual abandon. An onshore breeze made it a bit chilly as the sun went down, and I was the only one crazy enough to be outside, but some people were funny about dogs being in restaurants. Besides, the views of the sun setting over the river were gorgeous.

CAROLERS AND CORPSES

Propping my leg, I was mindlessly scrolling through my social media feed when Vincente DeMarco walked onto the patio, phone to his ear. We made eye contact, and he nodded before walking to the edge of the patio to look out at the water as he continued what sounded like an intense conversation.

My food arrived and I busied myself preparing a hamburger patty and sweet potato for The Colonel while trying not to listen as the CEO of DeMarco Canning Company ranted about deliveries being delayed and production being down.

I'd just bitten into my own burger when Vincente sat at the table across from mine and sighed, pocketing his phone. I glanced up to find him absently watching The Colonel clean his bowl.

Sitting back in his chair, he sighed again. Our gazes met and I offered a smile.

"Rough day?"

He grimaced. "Business as usual." He quirked a brow and tipped his head toward The Colonel. "He always eat that good?"

Chuckling, I shook my head. "Nah, only when it's passed his dinner time and we're stuck on an island."

Expecting him to laugh in commiseration, I blinked when he swore and launched into a diatribe about the causeway.

"... and after we worked so hard to raise the funds, that idiot Ross sabotaged us to keep his trophy tramp happy!"

Having just had a similar conversation with Felicity Simms, his reasoning wasn't a surprise. However, it did give me an opening to steer the conversation and knock another suspect interview off my list.

"Felicity Simms had similar sentiments when I spoke with her this afternoon."

A bark of humorless laughter erupted from Vincente. "I'll bet. That girl was brutal to Felicity."

"Mmm, so I gathered when I spoke with Justin Gambrell."

His lips twisted into a feral sneer. "That hack! Another colossal mess of Brianna Bellamy's making." He snorted. "Do you know she had the nerve to try and replace me as the soloist? Me! I've been the choir's lead tenor for almost a decade!"

Nodding, I waited for a beat and then pounced. "Yes, I understand you were very angry over her decision."

His eyes narrowed. "I was furious, so what?"

My brows rose. "Mad enough to kill?"

"What? Have you lost your mind?" He rose and slammed his hands onto my table, leaning forward so that his face was inches

CAROLERS AND CORPSES

from mine. A nerve ticked in his jaw. "That is a nasty insinuation and if you repeat it, I'll—"

"It was a simple question, and fair under the circumstances." I leaned back but didn't let my gaze waver. "What did you do when Brianna called a break?"

His nostrils flared and a vein throbbed in his temple. For a moment I worried he'd have a stroke but after a minute of heavy breathing he drew a long, deep breath and exhaled as he rose to full height. "You have some nerve." He snorted and started to walk away.

"Where were you during the break, Mr. DeMarco?"

"On a phone call with my plant manager, Daye." He stopped and looked over his shoulder. "Fair warning. If I hear you've been suggesting I'm in anyway involved in that woman's death you'll hear from my lawyer."

The door to the restaurant slammed shut as he stalked back inside. I released the breath I'd been holding and pushed my plate away; the charged conversation had soured my stomach.

I snapped The Colonel's leash to his collar and grabbed my bill. Hopefully, the tide had receded because, after antagonizing conversations with two of Gray's Island's residents it seemed prudent to beat a hasty retreat.

Chapter Twelve

The physical exertions of setting up the holiday market finally caught up to me, making my injured leg throb like a toothache. Coupled with the strain of finding a killer and clearing Madison's name, I spent a restless night tossing and turning. When the clock ticked over to six, I surrendered any idea of sleep and got up to face the day.

My mood was brighter after I managed to feed The Colonel and make a pot of tea without waking Mama. Arriving home from Gray's Island with an aching leg, a dog confused by the break in his routine, and a brain overloaded with too much information, all I'd wanted was a soak in the hot tub. But Mama had badgered me for information on the investigation and then launched into plans for Christmas. I'd had to plead a headache before I could retreat to my room.

Thankful for peace and quiet, I slipped out the front door and curled up on the porch swing while The Colonel explored the yard. Yesterday's conversations with Felicity Simms and Vincente DeMarco had confirmed what I already knew and given me new avenues to explore. Now, I needed to bring some order to the hodgepodge of information.

Reaching into the pocket of my cardigan, I pulled out an ink pen and the crumpled paper Connie and I had used to compile a list of suspects. I scrolled down the page until I found Felicity's name. Losing the position of choir director, Brianna seducing Felicity's husband, and being a horrible neighbor all went into the *Motives* column.

I tapped the pen against my front teeth, debating the likelihood that Brianna Bellamy lording it over the other women was a strong enough reason to kill. It seemed petty, but then, so did Brianna's stopping the causeway, but Felicity had mentioned it in her list of grievances. I added them to my list and moved on to Vincente.

He'd been angry over Bellamy replacing him as a soloist; angry but also offended, and wounded pride could be a powerful motivator. I scribbled that next to his name and then replayed our conversation. He'd gotten nasty when I asked him for his whereabouts when Brianna was killed.

The encounter had ended on an antagonistic note which had clouded my recollection but, in the cold light of a peaceful day, I remembered my shock at his reaction to my joke about being stuck on the island until the tide receded.

The DeMarco Canning Company was a wholesale distributor of canned seafood and, from what I'd overheard from his phone call, they were having trouble with deliveries. Considering his anger over Clayton Ross indulging his new bride by scuttling the causeway rebuild, was it a stretch to think Vincente would kill over it? Late or canceled deliveries could lead to a loss of customers which, in turn, would cause financial problems. Money or lack thereof was always a powerful motivator; I added it to my list.

Regardless of possible motives, both Felicity and Vincente had provided alibis for the probable time of Brianna's murder. I'd

CAROLERS AND CORPSES

need to confirm those and, since Valentina DeMarco was also a suspect, I could pay her a visit and kill two birds with one stone.

Whistling for The Colonel, I rose and headed to the front door. A text to my physical therapist had garnered an emergency appointment for later in the day, which left me time to complete a few of the tasks on Mama's holiday list. Stopping her nagging would allow me to concentrate on clearing Madison's name.

"Come on, buddy, let's go rustle Dewey from his bed."

It took more than an hour to motivate my brother and another thirty minutes was wasted while Mama hemmed and hawed over what needed to be done in preparation for celebrating the holidays, but Dewey and I were finally able to head to Petrie's Christmas Tree Farm.

The farm was bustling with customers. Many were friends and neighbors, but there was a definite coldness in some of the greetings and a few ignored me outright.

We chose a tree and I mentioned the tension I'd sensed as Dewey was paying the attendant.

He finished counting Dewey's change and then looked at me and laughed. "Half the county has been out here today and everyone is talking about the going's on at the holiday shindig."

My lips twisted as I scrunched my nose. "So, the gossip is all over town."

He snorted. "It's Sanctuary Bay. But it ain't just spreadin' around cuz people can't mind their business …" Puzzled, I frowned which made him laugh. "Ain't you watchin' the news? That's all they can talk about. Feels like the whole country is glued to the TV, wonderin' what'll come out next." He stepped closer and lowered his voice. "I saw that Neely gal's show last night. Somehow she got wind of Madison's fiancée foolin' around with that tart what got herself killed." He shook his head and sighed. "Gotta say, when I heard that … well, makes ya wonder is all I'll say."

I wanted to protest that innuendo and supposition weren't facts and that he shouldn't jump to conclusions, but thankfully,

CAROLERS AND CORPSES

Dewey dragged me away before I could build up a head of steam.

Tree purchased, we headed for Myrtlewood, stopping in route to pick up lunch from Frank's BBQ. After a quick bite, Madison and I got down to work, directing Dewey to set up the tree and hang the outdoor lights as Mama had instructed.

Madison was her happy and enthusiastic self, proving I'd made the right decision in hiding her at the plantation. No cable meant she wasn't seeing her personal life dissected on the national stage.

By the time I left for the gym, my leg was throbbing. I was dreading physical therapy but my trainer had drummed into me that being consistent was half the battle, so I dragged myself out to the truck and made my way back to Sanctuary Bay.

Lance greeted me with his typical cheer and proceeded to put me through my paces. After stretching and riding the recumbent bike, I moved to the leg press machine. My efforts over the past month had earned me the dubious honor of adding weight and each rep was a struggle.

Once Lance saw that I was holding the form he'd taught me, he walked across the room to chat with the desk clerk, leaving me to finish the set. With three reps completed, I was talking myself into the next when my thoughts drifted to the issue uppermost in my mind.

Felicity Simms had a laundry list of grudges against the victim, most centered around Brianna's lack of consideration for her neighbors, but Vincente DeMarco only had two motives as far as I could tell.

My investigation so far had centered around the idea that Brianna's death was linked to her treatment of the other carolers. That was still my most promising angle to explore, but both suspects had also mentioned Brianna's standing in the way of the causeway construction. I tightened my core and willed my thighs to move the metal plate away from my body but, still busy running through possible reasons someone would kill Brianna, my focus was divided. I shrieked as my legs were forced back toward my chest and the metal plate crashed back against the machine.

Lance was by my side in seconds.

"Hey, you all right?"

Shaking, and a bit unnerved, I drew a deep breath and nodded. "Yeah, yeah I'm okay, just got distracted."

He handed me my water bottle. "What did I tell you?" He continued to scold me as he walked around the machine and lowered the weight settings. "You've got to pay attention, you know? Keep your head in the game."

I licked my lips and pushed my bangs out of my face with a shaky hand. "I know. I just …" I shrugged because there was no good excuse.

Lance patted my shoulder. "It's hard, I know. But let me tell ya, if you don't keep your focus, it can set you back. I had this client, you might know her, Kay Emory?" I nodded and he continued. "Well, she started working with me about six months after the accident and we were making great progress. She got where she could stand, so we moved on to walking between the parallel bars. One day, she wasn't paying attention and lost her grip. Ended up on her butt. She was shaken, but otherwise fine, only …" Lance sighed and shook his head. "It scared her. She was afraid of reinjuring herself, of making her injuries worse so she quit coming all together. She'll be bound to that chair for the rest of her life if she doesn't work those muscles. Every so often I call her and try to coax her back but …"

My eyes widened. "I thought Kay's injuries were permanent."

"No, she bruised her spinal cord in the accident, but it's not severed. With therapy she could walk again, maybe not good as new, and probably not for long periods, but …" He sniffed.

"Probably shouldn't have, I mean, not supposed to talk about a client, confidentiality and all. Only, I wanted to make sure you know how important it is to keep at this and give it your full attention."

"Oh, yeah, I get it." I smiled. "And don't worry, I won't repeat what you said." I settled back at the machine and got into position for another rep. "I appreciate the pep talk, coach!"

Lance grinned. "Good. My job is done." He pointed at the leg press. "Now get back to work!"

Gritting my teeth, I followed his command. Unlike Kay Emory, I was determined to gain back my mobility and lose the cane.

Chapter Thirteen

My plan to check alibis was derailed when I called the cannery and found out Valentina DeMarco was out of the office. Since I'd also planned to talk to the plant manager during the trip, I decided to wait. Besides, PT, coupled with a lack of sleep, had taken a toll. A quick dinner, followed by a short walk for The Colonel, and I could be fast asleep before eleven o'clock.

I was wiping The Colonel's paws, how that dog managed to step in every speck of dirt was a mystery, when the irritating voice of Grace Neely reached my ears.

Giving The Colonel his teething bone, I stepped closer to the TV room and tuned in to what Neely was saying. It was one of those round table type discussions that always seemed to be scripted arguing to me. Neely's headshot was flanked by two people, both talking over one another in defense of their positions on the Bellamy murder case.

They were all so-called legal experts and could have been making good points but, once they started speculating on Madison's love life and relationship with her father, I was done listening.

Bidding Mama good night, I fell into bed and slept like the dead.

The next morning, I felt like a new woman, or at least one ready to take on whatever the day brought. I started with my DBT focus therapy. Scanning the room for a focusing object, my gaze skipped over the whistle I'd found the night Brianna was murdered.

Brannon had refused to consider it evidence and, upon reflection, I could concede his point. I made a mental note to drop it off at the market's lost and found and continued my search for something to practice DBT.

The therapy helped me stay grounded; several times I'd been on the verge of a panic attack. Between the focus therapy and The Colonel's stalwart presence, I'd calmed down and been able to function.

It also brought clarity. Using a mug of tea, I logged in my observations and sat back to consider Madison's case. As soon as I'd seen to The Colonel's needs, I was heading back to Gray's Island. Yesterday's conversation with Valentina's secretary confirmed she'd be in, but I'd declined the offer of an appointment. I wanted an element of surprise.

Confirming Felicity's alibi was first on my list and, by going to the cannery, I could also confirm Vincente's. After that, I needed to stop by the office. Not only did Connie need me to approve the revised centerpieces for the Osprey Point New Year's Eve party but I also needed some advice.

Tate had called and, because I knew what he wanted, I'd let it go to voice mail. Childish, but there it was. I needed to give him an answer on his invitation to the New Year's Eve celebration, and I was at a loss on how to turn him down and not ruin our friendship.

Business as usual for CoaStyle, a complex relationship, and finding a killer were all competing within my beleaguered brain and the latter problem had thrown up a complication I was wary of dwelling on. In order to investigate all my suspects, I could not avoid talking with Roland Dupree.

Since the nightmare I'd suffered after running into him, I'd managed to distract myself and remain free of the terror that seemed to haunt me, but I wasn't fool enough to believe I'd been miraculously cured. Avoidance at all costs had done more than the DBT or talking with my therapist.

Dr. Styles had warned me that the brain would seek its own level and that only by learning appropriate coping mechanisms could I achieve mental freedom.

An appointment with the good doctor was slated for tomorrow afternoon, but I'd toyed with the idea of canceling. I tried to avoid all thoughts of the shooting and my last nightmare had left me with an uneasy feeling. Something was off.

Common sense said not to take a dream too seriously; they could twist and distort reality. Yet what I'd seen just before waking did not make sense.

It nagged at me, my logical side wanted to dig deeper, to figure out *what* was bugging me. But, in order to do that, I'd have to willingly revisit what I did remember of that night and the very idea made my mouth go dry and my stomach roll.

A knock at my bedroom door got The Colonel barking, driving all other thoughts to the back of my mind. Mama was up and at them so everyone else would be, too.

"Colonel, calm down." I hopped off the bed and hollered. "Hold on, Mama, I'm comin'."

The house was old, my bedroom was relatively large, yet the sounds from The Colonel were deafening and I fussed until I reached the door. "Boy, sssh, it's just Mama."

I turned the knob, and he barreled through, wiggling and snorting, nearly knocking Mama over as he raced to the stairs.

"That dog!" Mama clucked and pursed her lips. "He needs training."

Since it was an old argument, I changed the subject. Mama could not understand that for an English bulldog, The Colonel *was* well trained; stubborn was built into his DNA. "Mornin' Mama, did you need something?"

She frowned and glanced at the now empty stairs. I could tell by the look on her face she wanted to finish scolding and complaining but, after a second, she met my gaze and sighed. "I was wondering if you were going into town. I'm due at Kitty's in an hour."

"Oh, well as soon as I've seen to the dog, I've got to go to DeMarco's Cannery but if you're getting your hair done, I should be back in time to pick you up."

Mama quirked an eyebrow. "What on earth are you going over there for?"

Without thinking, I blurted out my need to verify Felicity Simms and Vincente DeMarco's alibis and, like a shark smelling blood in the water, Mama pounced.

"Oh! Does that mean you think one of them killed that girl?"

I closed my eyes for a moment, accepting the blame for my own stupidity while I tried to formulate an answer that wouldn't be spread all over town before noon. "Um ... not, that is ..." I sighed and wondered how big a shovel I'd need to dig myself out of the mess I'd made.

Of all things, Mama was heading to the beauty parlor! Me and my stupid, stupid, stupid big mouth! "Look, Mama, you can't go spreading this around town."

Her shoulders went back. She looked at me and sniffed. "Why, I'm sure I don't know what you mean. I *never* gossip!"

CAROLERS AND CORPSES

Self-awareness was an incredible thing. Myriad replies were on the tip of my tongue, but I bit them all back; after all, I hadn't been raised a heathen and I had a healthy aversion to the punishment for disrespecting my elders. "Yes ma'am, of course not! I just meant we can't mention people's names as being linked to a murder. It's, um illegal and I could get sued."

I'd stretched the truth, but my reward was my mother taking it seriously. Her brows rose to her hair line, and she gulped. "Oh! We don't want that!" She raised her hand to her lips and simulated locking them. "I won't breathe a word, Holly Marie."

Somehow I doubted that, but I'd done my best and could only pray that by the time the rumors and innuendos reached the ears of Felicity Simms and Vincente DeMarco, they'd have been embellished so many times their origin would be a mystery.

Mama tried pumping me for information about the case a few more times but, when my lips remained sealed, she sighed and left me to dress in peace.

Traffic was snarled and by the time I dropped Mama at the beauty shop, it was past ten. I raced across town, but it still took me the better part of an hour and, once I got to the causeway, my stomach was rolling. Residential traffic was bad enough, but I couldn't imagine the road lasting much longer with all the semi traffic from the cannery.

Anxious that Valentina might leave for lunch, it wasn't until I pulled into the lot and saw her parking space was occupied that I relaxed. The receptionist directed me to the top floor. The Colonel and I entered the executive office wing where we were informed that Ms. DeMarco was in a meeting.

"I'm sorry, but without an appointment…"

Valentina's secretary was an older woman with a prim countenance. Used to dealing with difficult old ladies, I poured on the charm and after a few compliments she unbent and granted me ten minutes as soon as the meeting ended.

Settling The Colonel with his busy bone, I strolled around the waiting area. A bank of floor-to-ceiling windows ran the length of one wall, providing a breathtaking view of the harbor.

Shrimp boats pulled up to the dock and workers sprang into action, unloading the fragile cargo into rolling bins and ferrying them up the gangplank and in through large metal doors.

At an adjacent dock, oysters in burlap sacks were tossed onto a conveyor belt that disappeared inside the building. To the right of the pier, I could just make out a forklift operator shuttling to and from the bay doors, loading huge crates onto semis. Business seemed to be booming for the DeMarco family.

The sun came out from behind the clouds, driving me away from the windows. Looking for another distraction, a gallery wall drew me across the room.

Black framed photos chronicling the history of the cannery stood in stark relief against the white wall. My gaze wandered over images dating back to the early 1900s. A trio of children, not more than eight years old, shucking oysters and looking grim and worn. A wooden cart painted with the wares on offer and a smiling man in a white apron serving customers.

The images changed to full color, depicting the opening of the new wing and the appointment of Vincente as CEO. A group photo caught my attention. Flanked by Valentina and Vincente was Kay Emory, grinning from ear to ear and standing on her own two feet. It appeared to be a company picnic; the date was five years before her accident.

Seeing Kay in happier times was a grim reminder that life could change in the blink of an eye. I gave a word of thanks to God that my own injuries were less severe and permanent and turned my attention to artwork hanging farther along the wall.

A half dozen framed prints were arranged in two groupings. One set were clearly intended to be a series, with the first an artistic interpretation of the sunrise over the lighthouse that stood on the ocean side of Gray's Island. The second painting was a similar scene during a thunderstorm, and the last had been painted as if the artist had set up their easel on a boat, looking back at the lighthouse as the sun set over the island.

The paintings were stunning, the colors vibrant, and the brush strokes masterfully applied to capture the movement of the ocean. Continuing my perusal, I studied a scene depicting a pair of deer grazing at the edge of the dunes and another captured a blue heron rising from the marsh. The detail and clarity were astonishing; the talent of the artist apparent.

Wondering who the master was, my eyes widened as I caught sight of three tiny letters tucked into the lower right corner, colored to highlight the sea oats. VDm could only be Valentina DeMarco.

A door opened behind me. I turned to see Valentina striding toward me, looking every inch the CFO of a successful company.

"Holly! Sorry to keep you waiting, but it's a pleasure to see you. What brings you out this way?"

CAROLERS AND CORPSES

"Hello, thanks for seeing me on such short notice." I cocked my head and smiled. "I didn't get a chance to tell you how cute I thought your face painting was. I had no idea you were so talented."

I gestured to the heron and landscapes on the wall.

Valentina shrugged my praise aside, though it was obvious it pleased her. "It's nothing really. I studied for a while at the art school in Savannah but... it was not to be." Her smile was rueful. "The cannery has been in my family for over a hundred years. You know how it is."

I nodded because I did understand. Heritage, family, history—they were important in lots of places and cultures but in the South they were everything.

The business appeared to be thriving, leading me to assume she was good at her job, but I couldn't help but mourn the loss for what she might have done under different circumstances.

The Colonel waddled over, demanding to be pet and the conversation revolved around his royal cuteness for several minutes before Valentina straightened and asked me why I'd come.

Normally, I'd be subtle and ease the conversation where I needed it to go, but Valentina was a busy woman whom I guessed would appreciate the direct approach.

I cleared my throat. "Well, I'm looking into the murder of Brianna Bellamy, and I understand you were at choir practice that night."

Her posture stiffened and her eyes lost their shine. "Ah, you're checking Felicity's alibi." Her smile held no warmth. "She said you might."

Great, they'd gotten their stories synced. I cursed myself for not following up immediately. "Yes, I wanted to hear your impression of events that night and also confirm your whereabouts."

She quirked a brow. "You also spoke with my brother."

It wasn't a question, but I nodded anyway. "I ran into him while dining at the marina, yes."

Her lips pursed. "Should we retain counsel?"

It was my turn to raise my brows. "I'm asking unofficially, but you must do as you feel best."

Valentina held my gaze for a long moment. Just as my skin began to crawl, she relented, sitting back in her leather chair. "I'm given to understand you're prying into all of our lives in order to clear Madison Ross's name and send the police in a different direction?"

I nodded. "Madison isn't capable of murder."

"I see. But one of *us* is?"

I began to stumble my way through a response, but Valentina waved her hand, cutting off whatever I might have said. "I'll answer your questions, Ms. Daye, because I have nothing to hide. However, should my name, or that of my company, be bandied about in connection with this incident ..."

"I'll hear from your lawyer." My smile was tight. "Your brother has been there before you."

"Just so." She leaned forward and picked up an ornate letter opener, twirling it between her fingers. "I can verify that Felicity was walking along the river."

"Okay, do you know about what time it was when you joined her?"

Valentina's brow furrowed. "Let me see. We'd been kept waiting to begin practice and I checked my phone repeatedly during that time, so I know that Brianna Bellamy arrived at 11:13 p.m." She huffed. "The silly woman argued with Felicity for a good thirty minutes, ending with Fliss running off in tears." Valentina tapped the tip of the letter opener against the palm of her hand and nibbled at her lower lip. "Let me see, it was probably close to midnight—no! It was a few minutes after midnight when I went looking for Felicity. I remember because the bells chimed the hour."

"Okay, and how long was it before you caught up with Felicity?"

She blew out her breath and stared into the distance, considering my question. "Maybe ten minutes?"

I nodded. "You were with Felicity from about ten after midnight until when?"

"We walked to the end of the boardwalk. I calmed her down and then we retraced our steps and were headed to the parking lot when your brother prevented us from leaving. That must have been around one. After that, we were all assembled near the Christmas tree until you arrived."

Considering all that she said and plugging it in with what Justin Gambrell had told me, another question occurred to me. "You said Dewey gathered you all by the Christmas tree?" Valentina nodded. "Was everyone there at the same time? Or did he have to round them up?"

She cocked her head to the side. "I think we were all there within minutes of each other—Roland Dupree, that pop singer friend of Brianna's, and Kay Emory returned last—oh no, Gary was last to arrive."

CAROLERS AND CORPSES

Speaking to Gary was already a priority, now I had to put Roland Dupree there, too. Of course, it'd be him. I drew a deep breath and fought a queasy feeling in my gut. I didn't relish talking to him, much less asking pointed questions that Valentina's statement raised.

Justin Gambrell's whereabouts were easily confirmed by visiting Pug Ziggler's convenience store, besides, he didn't have a motive that I could see.

That left Kay, whose infirmities made her an unlikely murderer, and Gary Walston. I'd have to pursue those leads, but first I'd speak with the plant manager and check Vincente's alibi.

I rose from my chair and offered my hand. "Thank you for your time, Valentina. You've been very helpful."

"Happy to. I assume you are speaking with the other choir members?"

My hand was on the doorknob but something in the way she posed the question made me pause and look over my shoulder. Valentina watched me through narrow eyes. She continued to toy with the lethal looking letter opener and her expression was calculating.

"Yes. Your brother claims to have been speaking with your plant manager during the break. After I've confirmed that, I will be speaking with Roland Dupree, Kay Emory, and Gary Walston." I paused and quirked a brow. "Is there someone else you feel should be on my list?"

Her lips twisted into a smirk. "No, but do you know why Brianna called for a break?"

Justin had said the break was called after everyone started complaining about Brianna's treatment of Felicity. I repeated that to Valentina.

She chuckled. "Oh, we were all miffed at her rude and childish behavior but one of us took it a bit further." When I didn't rise to her baited statement, Valentina pinned me with a challenging stare. "I would think a shouting match, complete with cursing and wild gesticulations warrants a closer look."

I pursed my lips, tired of the cat and mouse game. "It would, if I knew who you were describing."

Her brows raised and a tight smile stretched her lips. "Why, Gary Walston, of course."

Chapter Fourteen

The conversation with Valentina left a sour taste in my mouth. I was at a loss to pinpoint exactly what she'd said or done to cause it, but I couldn't leave the cannery fast enough. With help from Valentina's secretary, I was able to meet with the plant manager, confirm Vincente's alibi, and drive out of the gates in under thirty minutes.

Shifting into second gear, I fell into place behind a line of tractor trailers and let my thoughts drift. The meeting with Mark

Lomax had been straightforward—flooding on the causeway had caused an important shipment to be late and a valued client was hot under the collar. He'd thought it urgent enough to call his boss after midnight.

The reason for the early morning call was a strong motive for Vincente. Absent from anything else, I felt comfortable moving him to the bottom of my suspect list but, something Lomax had said in passing gave me pause.

He'd mentioned how exacting of a boss Vincente was as the reason he'd called him instead of dealing with it himself. Lomax was new to the job. The company had employed three people in as many years and, according to him, management did not give him unqualified support.

"No one lives up to Saint Emory."

I'd guessed who he was alluding to and had it confirmed. Kay Emory was the previous plant manager. She'd resigned because of her accident. It was a throwaway comment as it pertained to Vincente's guilt or innocence, but it got me thinking about Kay and the happy photo I'd noticed outside of Valentina's office.

Kay Emory didn't rank high as a suspect, or she hadn't. Aside from her being present during the estimated time of Brianna's death, she was confined to a wheelchair. I couldn't see her being physically able to restrain a woman as young and fit as Brianna Bellamy, much less have the necessary hatred to viciously murder her by means of expandable faux snow powder.

However, learning that she'd been plant manager started me thinking about why she no longer held the position. It all boiled down to a faulty road. The accident on the causeway had cost her a son, the use of her legs, and a successful career. Brianna Bellamy had been fighting against the new road; there was no denying Kay had motive.

As I inched my way through traffic, I weighed the pros and cons of Kay being the killer. In the end, I sided with the cons. Regardless of motive, Kay was the least likely to have killed Brianna because she didn't have full mobility and nothing physically linked her to the scene of the crime.

Gary Walston, on the other hand, had motive, physical evidence, and proximity. He would remain my primary suspect, unless he could provide an iron clad alibi. Kay was near the bottom of my list but that was no reason not to speak with her and, as I was already on the island ... Decision made, I turned right at the stop sign and drove toward the interior of Gray's Island and the subdivision the Emorys' called home.

Aside from the waterfront custom homes and a small, gated community adjacent to the marina, Gray's Island had been left natural, with a handful of modest ranch style houses scattered amidst the maritime forest and wetlands. The Emorys' small ranch style home was one of three situated on a dead-end dirt road.

I parked next to Kay's converted van and set The Colonel down. After a few minutes waiting for him to take care of business, we walked up the ramp and knocked on the door. Several minutes passed with no response. I was turning to leave when I caught movement through the frosted glass.

My eyes widened, and my hand reached for the service weapon that used to reside at my hip. A man carrying a rifle cracked the door and peered through.

Tense and ready to take cover, I relaxed as our gazes met and David Emory flashed a warm smile. "Holly Daye, what a pleasant surprise!" He let the door swing wide and motioned for me to step through.

"Mornin' David." I tipped my head toward his hand. "You always come to the door loaded for bear?"

He snorted and leaned the gun against the hall table. "Sorry about that. We're pretty isolated out here and the neighbor's four-wheeler was stolen last week." He shrugged. "We're all on alert."

"Sorry to hear that."

He sighed. "Yeah, what's the world comin' to? But, come on in, make yourselves comfortable." He bent and patted The Colonel's head and then tilted his head toward an archway that led into the living room where a news program was blaring. From the grating accent, I assumed it was the Legal News Network.

David sank into a worn, tweed recliner and reached for the remote. Grace Neely's face faded to black, and the room was mercifully silent. "What brings y'all out this way?"

I perched on the edge of a shabby brown sofa and commanded The Colonel to sit at my feet before replying. "Oh, I had business at the cannery and thought we'd swing by and visit Kay. She around?"

He smiled. "Sure is, hang on and I'll get her." He shuffled off toward the back of the house, calling for his wife.

David hadn't been gone for more than a minute when a door slammed somewhere in the house. The Colonel growled and jumped up, knocking into the end table and sending a cluster of framed photographs tumbling to the floor.

"Crap! Colonel, sit down!" I knelt and gathered the items; thankful nothing had broken. I was setting the frames back in place when one photo caught my eye.

A blonde-haired boy, dressed in a black-and-white referee's uniform, was standing on a soccer field with a team of preschool-aged children. He was holding something silver toward the camera and grinning from ear to ear.

Aaron David Emory had been one week shy of his thirteenth birthday when the car accident took his life. If I had to guess, the picture was taken not long before he died. My heart broke for Kay and David.

"He'd just won Referee of the Year."

I glanced up as David entered the room. "I'm so sorry."

He sniffed. "Thanks. It's ... well, you know." He sighed and dragged a hand through his hair. "Um, Kay is laying down. I told her you were here, but she's taken her pill and is half out of it."

"Oh, no problem. I can come back another time." I rose and nudged The Colonel to his feet. "You said she'd taken medicine. Is Kay ill?"

David shook his head and started walking toward the door. "Nah, it's this anxiety medicine? Maybe a sleeping pill. I can't remember what it's for, but that Elavil is strong stuff, she'll be out for hours."

"Well, we won't keep you then." I clicked my tongue. "Come on, Colonel, time to pick up Mama."

"Give Ms. Effie my love."

"Will do!" The Colonel insisted on exploring the sidewalk and detouring to a line of hedges, but in a few minutes we were approaching the causeway. The dashboard clock showed it'd be another hour before Mama was ready. Just enough time to swing by the Walston residence.

Chapter Fifteen

The Walstons made their home in The Preserve, an affluent gated community situated on Adler Creek in the north end of Noble County. Years of serving court documents gained me entrance. The guard gave me a cheery wave and pointed me in the right direction, no questions asked.

The Preserve was designed to blend in with the surrounding wetlands and forest. It wasn't unusual to come upon a gator lumbering across the road or see shore birds in the many lagoons that dotted the neighborhoods. Gary's home turned out to be two doors down from the house where The Colonel's dognappers had been busted.

Nestled amidst a yard of pines and azaleas, the Walstons had an elevated Lowcountry styled home with waterfront access. I parked the Scout next to a trailered deep-V boat sporting a for sale sign. As The Colonel and I approached the front door, we passed a four-passenger mule and two jet skis also for sale; all signs pointed to Gary being in financial trouble.

Gary stepped onto the porch as we came up the walk. "Hey Holly, saw y'all pull in. What brings you out this way?"

"Hey Gary, can't stay long, gotta pick Mama up at the Kut and Kurl."

He snorted. "Women and their hair; she'll be there all day, have a seat."

I settled The Colonel and sank onto the rocking chair beside his. "Too true, but she promised to be finished by one. If I get there at one thirty …"

Gary laughed and unwrapped a piece of gum. "Sound strategy. Can't tell you how many times I've cooled my heels waitin' on MaryAnn." He chomped on the gum for a few seconds and then asked, "What have you been up to, then? Holiday market doin' good?"

"Yeah, had a little issue with a strand of the lights your crew installed, but other than that I haven't heard of any problems; well, aside from finding Brianna Bellamy dead."

"Bad business, that. Can't believe what the TV is saying. No way little Maddie Ross could do such a thing." His brow furrowed. "But you said something went wrong with the lights?"

"Uh-huh. You didn't check them Sunday night?" I watched him for any signs of discomfort, but his body language remained open and relaxed.

"Sunday? No, I turned that job over to Bob and his crew." He frowned. "He's always been reliable, does good work. I'm sorry if—"

"No worries, and you did the install out of pocket, we are all grateful. Bob happened to be at the market with his family when someone complained that a strand near the craft tents wasn't working. He got a ladder and checked it. Thing is"—our gazes met, and I kept eye contact as I added—"one of the bulbs was loose."

Again, Gary didn't squirm, fidget, or look away. He was a great liar or there was another reason for finding the wrapper of his distinctive gum by the lamp post. It was time to be direct. "While Bob was checking the strand, I searched the area and found a Clove gum wrapper right beside the pole. Yet you say you haven't been near the posts?"

He sat up straighter and frowned. "I told you I let the crew handle the job. Had no reason to go behind them. I'm sorry if they did shoddy work, I'll speak to them."

His voice was cool, and his body language told me he was getting wary. Under normal circumstances, I'd have apologized but, these weren't normal times. "The crew did a fine job, Gary, and like I said, everyone is grateful. Bob explained that those kinds of lights only work when all the bulbs are connected." I paused, holding his gaze. "I'm thinking someone unscrewed one of the bulbs and, since they were working fine throughout opening night, it had to have been done after the park closed."

He frowned. "Why would someone—oh!" His eyes widened. "You think it has something to do with the murder?"

I nodded. "Madison Ross told me she returned to the park around midnight. She was looking for her sewing bag and mentioned that it was dark by the tent, so it seems logical to assume the bulb was loosened for that reason."

"Whew, that's ... cold. You think someone planned to kill her?"

"Looks that way."

Gary shook his head and sighed. "Who would do such a thing? I mean, she was annoying but ... I can't believe Maddie had that kinda anger in her."

"Neither can I, which is why I'm looking for the real killer."

His brows rose. "Any leads?"

Watching him closely, I dropped the proverbial other shoe. "A Clove gum wrapper was found beside the lamp post."

"Wha—are you implying I killed her?"

His face was turning a mottled red, but I refused to respond to his anger. Keeping my tone neutral, I opted to ignore his question in favor of my own. "What did you do after your argument with Brianna?"

Gary's mouth dropped open. He sputtered like a fish for a second before finding his voice. "There was no argument. I don't have to take this in my own home! I want you to leave."

"I will, after you've answered the question." I rose and gathered The Colonel's leash until he was standing beside me. "Numerous people have stated that you and Brianna got into it after Felicity stormed off. They've said you laid into her for upsetting

CAROLERS AND CORPSES

Felicity along with some other things. Brianna got angry and called for a break and everyone went in different directions. So, where did you go and what did you do?"

Chest rising and falling in rapid jerks, Gary scowled and looked away. Unfazed, I waited until his breathing evened out and pressed for an answer. "Gary? Where did you go during the break?"

"The bathroom! Satisfied?" He jumped up and began to pace. "I can't believe ... you have some nerve, insinuating I killed that witch." He stomped across the porch, muttering. "Why would you think I—?" Hands on hips, he turned and met my gaze. Puzzlement was clear on his face, but the edge of anger was still apparent in his posture. "You're accusing me of murder because of a piece of paper laying on the ground? Anyone could have dropped that, heck, it could have been there for days!"

"Not just any paper, Gary. You chew Clove gum and you admitted to using it to fight the urge to smoke." I quirked a brow. "The wrapper isn't faded or wrinkled. The sprinklers came on that night. If it'd been there earlier it wouldn't be crisp and bright red."

"But why would I kill her? I have no reason."

"Rumor has it, your company has money problems. Problems that would be solved if you got the Gray's Island Causeway job, and Brianna Bellamy was holding that project up."

He sputtered. "What? I'm not—who told you that? My company is doing fine!"

Tilting my head towards the drive, I shrugged. "Trying to sell a lot of toys ..."

"So? We don't use—"

"Gary, you're an avid fisherman and you have a deep-water dock."

"That means nothing, I'm upgrading and ..." The look on my face must have shown how little I was buying what he was trying to sell. His words trailed off on a sigh as his shoulders drooped. "Okay, so money is tight." His lower lip jutted out. "But I didn't kill her!"

"Then you won't mind telling me where you were during the break."

Eyes flat, Gary glared at me. "I was talking with Roland Dupree. Now get off my property and don't come back!"

He stalked into the house without a backward glance, leaving me to accept the fact that I was leaving a trail of angry friends

CAROLERS AND CORPSES

behind and, worse, no matter how I tried to convince myself otherwise, I now couldn't avoid speaking with Roland Dupree.

Chapter Sixteen

Dinner with Mama at the Country Kitchen, complete with non-stop commentary on the private lives of almost everyone in Sanctuary Bay, did little to distract me from the meeting I dreaded. Throughout our meal, my mind replayed the scene in the park and the feelings that unplanned meeting had dredged to the surface.

A lifetime of learning to tune out Mama's chatter had served me well while we were in public, but once alone, I'd been help-

CAROLERS AND CORPSES

less to halt the flashbacks. The Colonel's comforting warmth had warded off a full-blown panic, attack but it took ages to fall asleep and, when my body finally gave in, I'd fallen into another bad dream.

The flashbacks and nightmares were nothing new. Through therapy, I was learning to cope with the endless revisiting of that terror-filled night. But the nightmares I'd experienced since running into Shawn Dupree's father were different.

Before, the flashbacks replayed the long drive through the hunting camp, culminating in me exiting the car and being shot. What I was dreaming about now started with that familiar refrain but added the moments that I lay injured and praying for help.

According to the police report, I'd seen Shawn, stopped the car, and attempted to serve him with the court summons. He'd raised his hunting rifle and fired a split second before I returned fire, killing him instantly.

The trouble was my dream didn't follow that narrative. I'd studiously avoided remembering that night, partly out of fear it would bring on a panic attack, but also because Dr. Styles advised against forcing the memories. She'd said my brain was protecting itself, and when I was ready, the full memory might return.

Having suffered at the hands of what little I did remember, and losing consciousness on a few occasions, I'd been content to let well enough alone. But now ...

"Dr. Styles will see you now."

I glanced up and made eye contact with the young man sitting behind the reception desk. He smiled and nodded toward the office door. I prodded The Colonel into motion, and we entered the inner office.

Handing him his busy bone, I settled into the leather recliner opposite Dr. Styles' chair.

"Good morning, Holly. Ready for the holidays?"

A sardonic reply would have been more truthful, but I gave a perfunctory answer and waited for her to start our session. The ticking of a mantle clock harmonized with The Colonel's gnawing for several minutes as the doctor perused my file.

My gaze roamed the room, examining the familiar artwork and fighting the urge to fill the silence with mindless chatter. I'd begun to fidget when she closed the folder and pushed her reading glasses to the top of her head.

"Now then, since Thanksgiving, we've stretched the time between our appointments to every other week. How has that worked for you? Any problems or incidents where you've lost control?"

Her smile, polite but distant, always grated on my nerves. She came highly recommended, but the lack of a bedside manner made my visits something to endure as a condition of the disability insurance and not a place to share my thoughts and concerns.

Usually, I told her what she wanted to hear, but the unexpected meeting with Roland Dupree and the knowledge that I would have to initiate another was weighing on me. I needed to address the feelings that had been dredged from my subconscious.

I cleared my throat and gathered my thoughts. "I ran into Roland Dupree at the holiday market Sunday night."

Her expression remained bland. Nothing of what she was thinking showed in her eyes or body language; being unable to read her was my biggest qualm about seeing her.

She held my gaze for a few seconds and then tilted her head to the side. "How did that make you feel?"

"I ..." My mouth went dry, and a wave of emotions clamored for attention. I tried to shy away from them, but the feelings were too strong. "Scared. I, uh ran away from him."

"I see. What were you afraid of?"

And that was the bargain bin question. Why had I run from him? Roland had done nothing. A polite greeting and I'd frozen, then rushed away.

My mind went back to that moment. I tried to observe the scene with detachment and articulate what had been going through my mind.

"I remember thinking how much he'd changed." I looked up and locked eyes with Dr. Styles. "I've known Roland Dupree socially for years. He always looked like he stepped off the cover of a men's magazine, even playing tennis or golfing. Yet Sunday night his clothes were shabby, his hair mussed, he needed to shave."

"He was in the park, maybe that's why he was dressed casually."

I shook my head. "No, Roland was a snazzy dresser all the time, and a social occasion like the holiday market? The Roland I knew would have been dressed to impress."

She nodded, conceding my point. "Then it was out of character. Why did it bother you?"

Why did it? I swallowed past a lump in my throat and forced myself to address the real issue. "Because ..." I sighed and surrendered to the feelings begging to be expressed. "Because the change in him is my fault."

Dr. Styles' brow furrowed. "Why would you assume that?"

"Oh, come on, everything about him screams sadness! He's devastated by the loss of Shawn and that is entirely my fault."

"That bothers you."

Her statement gave me pause. The normal answer would be not just yes, but heck yes! Yet, how I felt about taking Shawn Dupree's life was not normal. In fact, my feelings on the matter were at the root of my current struggles. I considered the emotions, or lack thereof, debating how much to confess.

Minutes passed before I mustered the courage to tell the truth. "Actually, I don't feel anything." I searched her face for signs that I was a horrible person, beyond the pale, and worthy of being cast away from polite society. What I read was typical of the doctor, unemotional and detached. It made my blood boil.

"For crying out loud, I've just confessed to being a monster and you sit there looking like butter wouldn't melt in your mouth! What is wrong with you?"

My outburst should have provoked a normal person to respond in kind, but Dr. Styles was as cool as a cucumber. I had to hand it to her, her training had sunk deep, or she was one cold fish.

Her blank stare unnerved me, but also served to diffuse my anger. We sat in tense silence for several minutes until I reached the limit of my patience. "Well? Nothing to say?"

"What would you like me to say?"

I rolled my eyes. "I don't know. How about, Holly Daye, you ought to be ashamed of yourself! Or you are a vile human being, and no decent person should ever associate with you again?"

"Is that how you feel? Unfit for civilized society? That you should be punished for your actions?"

My eyes widened. "Shouldn't I feel that way? I took a man's life!"

"In defense of your own."

And there it was, the root I'd been mentally tripping over. "Was it, though?"

CAROLERS AND CORPSES

Her brows rose and I gave myself a point for having goaded her into even a slight reaction.

"Are you saying that you don't feel the shooting was justified?"

"I don't know what I'm saying." The words popped out of my mouth before I thought about them, but once uttered I had to consider.

Was the issue that I didn't think I had a right to defend myself or was it that my memories suggested I hadn't shot in self-defense?

"Since my encounter with Roland, I've been having this dream—nightmare really." My reply was hesitant, letting my mind dance around the edges of the reoccurring dream as I searched for words.

"Tell me about it."

Mouth dry, I stared at the wall behind her head and let the images come. "It's the usual drive through the woods. I can smell the pines and a hint of pluff mud." I glanced over and met her eyes. "I remember thinking the tide is going out and I saw a boat approaching the hunting camp's dock as I drove over the Cypress Creek bridge. If they didn't hurry, they'd get stuck in the pluff mud." I shrugged away the irrelevant fact and continued. "The camp is a rabbit warren of dirt roads, and I've no idea which way to turn when I come to a fork. I stop. While I'm deciding on left or right, a shot rings out. It sounds close so I turn left, figuring Roland or Shawn has bagged a deer."

Disjointed images flashed before my eyes and my pulse began to race as I allowed myself to actively recall what happened after I made that fateful turn. It was a testament to Dr. Styles' therapy that I'd gotten that far without panicking but now ... I gulped and stared at the floor, willing my heart to slow to a normal rhythm.

"Are you all right? Do you need a break?"

My head jerked as she broke the silence, but her words allowed me to focus on something other than the edge of the dark abyss I was hovering near. "I ... um," I swallowed a few times and cleared my throat. *You can do this, Holly. Just breathe and let it out.*

The mental pep talk did little more than distract me but, following my own instructions, I drew several deep breaths and stroked The Colonel's wiry coat. It took a few minutes, but I was able to continue. "The sun is almost down, and the tree cover is dense. I flicked on the high beams and slowed to a crawl." I glanced at Dr. Styles, and she nodded.

"Good, if you feel able, tell me what happened next."

CAROLERS AND CORPSES

"There's a curve in the road, I come out of it and there's a pickup truck up ahead. Its lights are on. There's something laying in front of the truck, I can't ... I think it must be a deer because it's big, stretching the length of the front end."

A tremor ran through me as the scene continued to play in my head. My voice dropped to a whisper as I tried to explain what I was seeing. "I can see people standing beside the truck, I roll to a stop, and park the car. Something makes me leave it running." I shivered as gooseflesh broke over my body. My stomach started to roll, and bile rose in my throat.

"Holly? That's enough." Dr. Styles leaned in and patted my leg. "That's the most you've ever been able to tell me. How are you feeling?"

Bad, shaky, like I wanted to puke. I hated it, despised being so weak and helpless, a slave to a memory. I shook my head and ran a hand through my hair. This had to end. I told Dr. Styles as much and her brows rose.

"We've talked about this. The mind is a complex organism, it will take time to heal. You're able to revisit parts of that day without lapsing into a state of panic. It's progress."

"Maybe, but now there's the nightmare." I sniffed and thought of what I'd seen in my dream. My heart started beating faster and acid churned in my stomach. I clutched at The Colonel's warm body, making him snort and jerk awake.

"Sorry, buddy." He rose, stretched, and scooted closer to sit between my legs. Grateful, I leaned over and wrapped my arms around his neck, laying my head on top of his. He was a lifesaver, in more ways than one.

"Let's change the subject."

I lifted my head and met her gaze. "What? Why? I have to do something about this new dream." I took a shuddering breath. "I'm afraid to close my eyes. I never know if or when it'll happen again. And don't get me started on my guilt." I snorted. "Or should I say the lack of guilt?"

Dr. Styles nodded and sat back. "I can prescribe—"

"No!" Her eyes widened and I realized I'd shouted. I drew a deep breath, calmed myself, and tried to explain. "I don't want to be dependent on drugs. If I could just …" I huffed and looked at Dr. Styles. "Something is wrong. Why don't I feel guilty?"

"Should you feel that way? You shot in self-defense. Why are you questioning that, by the way. The report is very clear about what happened."

I shrugged. "I'm not sure, it's something about this new flashback … something doesn't add up and it's hounding me."

CAROLERS AND CORPSES

"Dreams can often be an amalgamation of what we see and do in our conscious hours combined with things our subconscious has absorbed without our awareness. It's best not to read too much—"

"It's keeping me awake at night, I need to know why it's bothering me!"

Dr. Styles stiffened and sat up straight. Her gaze flitted away toward the window for a second before she licked her lips and looked back at me. "As I've said, the brain will compensate for trauma by withholding information until you're able to process."

I snorted. "Well, I need to process it now because I'm desperate for a full night's sleep, and I have to speak with Roland Dupree on another matter. I can't run away every time I encounter him!" I dragged a hand through my hair and huffed. "If I could just make myself remember!"

"Oh, don't do that!"

The doctor's outburst made me focus on her and, for the first time since I'd met her, she was reacting to something I said. Eyes wide, Dr. Styles had leaned forward in her chair. She clutched an ink pen with a white-knuckled grip and every few seconds she'd catch her lower lip between her teeth; trained to read body language, my internal alarm started clanging.

I frowned, ready to ask the good doctor a few questions but The Colonel pawed my leg. I commanded him to lay down and when I looked again she was sitting back, relaxed, and wearing the familiar mask.

She glanced at the clock. "Holly, our session is almost over, and I think we should stop here. Let me congratulate you on your progress and wish you a happy Christmas."

My brows shot up to my hairline as I snorted. "Progress? I don't think anything was accomplished today!"

Her lips twisted into a parody of a smile. "It's common to feel that way but let me assure you that being able to extend the time between sessions without succumbing to your anxiety is a good thing, and you were able to tell me a little of what happened. That's a breakthrough."

Considering what I'd been able to talk about, I conceded the point but raised another. "I am happy about that but ..." I frowned, trying to find the right way to relay my concerns. "What about the nightmare? I have to speak with Roland Dupree. What if it makes the nightmare worse? If I could just figure out what I saw after I was shot—"

"Holly! Stop dwelling on that."

Her tone was sharp and, looking closer, I noticed she was again worrying at her lower lip. My eyes narrowed. That was the second time she'd dropped her professional armor.

She cleared her throat and glanced at the coffee table. "It's best not to force these things, the memories will come when you're ready. Our next session can address whether what you're dreaming is fiction or reality. In the meantime, remember the subconscious can play tricks."

I bit my lip, thinking of what I'd dreamed and comparing it to the times I'd suffered from other flashbacks. "I've thought of all that, but this isn't like a weird dream you get after eating spicy food. The emotions are real, it replays the same as every other flashback, only there's a part that is new and it scares me so much that I wake up. Why would my mind suddenly make things up?" My hand curled into a fist, and I slammed it on the arm of the recliner. "If only I could make myself remember!"

A gasp made me raise my head. I found Dr. Styles watching me. She was poised on the edge of her chair and a wary look was in her eyes. I frowned.

What was going on? In all the months I'd been seeing her, this was the first time I'd seen her be other than clinically professional. "Is something wrong? You seem bothered by me talking about this."

Her mask slid back into place as she donned her glasses. "Not at all and I apologize if I've given you that impression. You must feel free to discuss anything with me." Her look was expectant but otherwise I saw nothing remarkable about her behavior. I shrugged and nodded. Maybe I'd imagined it.

Dr. Styles flashed a bright smile, and her voice was chipper as she continued. "Now then, looking at your journal, I see that you've been doing DBT consistently. I believe your success can be attributed to the practice so continue to do that and we'll talk again in the New Year. I'll be out of the office from December twenty-second until January ninth, so let's set an appointment for later in that week." She rose and offered her hand. "But should you suffer another panic episode and need to talk, don't hesitate to text me."

I wanted to argue but the timer that clocked our sessions chimed. Besides, her refusal to let me address my latest memories irritated me. Aggravation must have shown on my face because Dr. Styles paused while opening the office door.

"In light of what we've discussed today, I feel I should caution you about forcing the memories. Doing so could set back the progress you've made. You mentioned this new memory appeared directly after seeing Roland Dupree. It might be coincidence, but to be on the safe side, if you can, avoid being in his proximity, and I advise against initiating contact."

Waking The Colonel, I exited the office and stopped by the receptionist to set my next appointment out of habit.

The doctor's parting advice, coupled with her comments during our session didn't sit well with me.

If I wanted to clear Madison's name, I had to continue looking for Brianna Bellamy's killer. To do that, I had to speak with Roland Dupree. I couldn't avoid him. Dr. Styles wouldn't approve, but last time I checked, I didn't need her permission.

Chapter Seventeen

The confidence I'd felt upon leaving Dr. Styles' office dissipated as I drove toward Roland Dupree's law office. My first avoidance technique was to slow down, but after a few indignant drivers honked at me, I was forced to resume the customary speed limit and arrived far quicker than was comfortable.

Sitting in the car thinking about what I needed to accomplish with Roland allowed me to procrastinate for another fifteen minutes, but all too soon, I reached the point of no return. I either walked inside or ran away.

Since I despised that weakness in myself, I sucked it up and forced myself into action. Getting The Colonel out of the Scout took a few more minutes, but I still found myself facing the firm's receptionist sooner rather than the later I'd have preferred.

"I'd like to speak with Mr. Dupree, if he has a few minutes free."

Please don't be available, be in court, be with a client, be on a conference call ...

"As it happens, Mr. Dupree is between meetings at the moment." The well-dressed young man gave me a practiced smile. "Who shall I say is calling?"

My breath caught and I had to swallow several times before I could mumble a reply, but I forced the words out and watched with trepidation as my last glimmer of reprieve circled the drain.

The receptionist hung up the phone and rose. "If you'll follow me?"

Walking the short distance to Roland's office was like taking my final steps before facing Old Sparky. The Colonel's nails tapped a tattoo on the heart pine floors. I counted the rhythmic tip-tapping beats in my head and synced my breaths with every forward step he took.

My buddy's presence once again provided an anchor to my swirling emotions, and I was able to enter the double doors with a modicum of calm. Meeting Roland's puzzled gaze however made my mouth go dry and I gratefully jumped at the offer of coffee.

The silence was thick and awkward as we sat waiting for the receptionist to return.

Roland sat back in his leather chair, fingers steepled across his chest, a slight smile hovering on his lips. It made my skin crawl. I drew a deep breath, leaned down to stroke The Colonel's back, and fought my fight-or-flight reflex.

Keeping my gaze down, I studied Roland from under my lashes. The shabby clothes from Sunday night had been replaced with casual slacks and a button-down shirt. It was still a far cry from the natty clothes he had been known to wear a year ago, but at least they were clean. He'd also shaved, and his color was better, though the light in his eyes was still dim.

I had a horrible suspicion that the change in Roland could be attributed to his grief and, despite not feeling guilty for killing his son, I wasn't so lacking in decency that I couldn't empathize with the pain he was obviously suffering.

Rattling china announced the arrival of coffee and several minutes were filled with generic questions on how I took it. Once we'd run through those mundane topics, I was at a loss on how to proceed; Roland took that problem from me.

Setting his cup on the desk, he smiled and made eye contact. "It's nice to see you, Holly, but I'm assuming after our brief encounter at the park you aren't here for social purposes."

I sucked in a breath. Roland hit hard and fast: he got straight to the point *and* managed to get in a subtle jab. I'd been married to a lawyer for thirty years, why was I surprised?

Fighting against my inner coward, I forced myself to match Roland's style. "I need to speak with you about the events surrounding the murder of Brianna Bellamy." A pause for air and I was able to address the elephant in the room. "About the other night, I apologize. I uh, wasn't expecting to, that is ... I'm sorry for your loss, Roland."

A twitch of the nerve in his cheek was the only sign that my apology had affected him. I braced myself for his response.

After a minute of silence, he cleared his throat and nodded. "There are many things I'd like to say, but good manners suggest a thank you is sufficient." He leaned forward and glanced at the planner occupying one corner of his executive desk. "I'm afraid I have a prior commitment and must leave in ten minutes. What can I tell you about that night that I haven't told the police, and why should I speak to you on this subject?"

Since I hadn't seen any official statements I couldn't answer his question directly, but I had a few of my own. "You don't have to answer my questions, of course, but I'm making inquiries on behalf of Madison Ross, and we'd appreciate your cooperation."

Roland quirked a brow and smirked. "You don't believe Ms. Ross is guilty."

"Do you?"

A flash of amusement sparked in his blue eyes. "I must confess that, although I haven't bothered to examine the particulars of the case, my gut instinct would be no, Madison Ross did not kill Brianna Bellamy." He sipped his coffee. "What can I do to assist you in your endeavor?"

Before the events that changed our lives, I'd liked Roland. He was erudite and had a dry sense of humor that could make a dull dinner party filled with legal eagles tolerable. I nudged the elephant back into its box and pretended I was talking to the Roland I'd known before his son had been killed by my hand.

"I've talked to several other choir members, could you start by telling me your version of what occurred after the park closed?"

Roland reiterated what I'd learned from Justin Gambrell and finished with Brianna Bellamy calling for a break. "And that was the end of choir practice because she never returned. Everyone filtered back to the stage about twenty minutes later and we stood around, wondering where Brianna was for a few minutes." He took a sip of coffee and continued. "Around ten minutes to one, Vincente started making noises about going home, the others picked up the refrain, and it was decided we should call it a night. We were heading to the parking lot when Dewey stopped us and requested we assemble near the Christmas tree and wait for further instructions. We were in the dark until you showed up." He snorted. "Your brother refused to explain why we were required to stay."

Refraining from commenting on Dewey's handling of the situation, I pressed on. The conversation was civil, if stilted, and I was far from comfortable in his presence. "Were you present when Gary Walston took Brianna to task over her treatment of Felicity?"

Roland nodded. "Indeed, I was. Best laugh I've had in ages." A genuine smile lit his face. "I offered to buy him a drink."

An answering smile stretched my lips before I could stop it. "And is that what you did during the break?"

He shook his head. "Unfortunately, no. It was early morning, and the bars were all closed. Besides, at that point we thought practice would continue once the women got themselves under control."

Roland's answer reeked of condescension but, considering what had transpired that night I figured the sisterhood deserved the hit and let it pass. "Then what did you do? Were you with Gary?"

"Ah, that's why you're here. Gary claimed me as his alibi."

Roland Dupree's statement proved that, despite his grief, he retained a sharp legal mind. "He has. Can you confirm he was with you during the break?"

He cocked his head to the side and quirked a brow. "Now that depends."

I frowned. His tone held a taunting note. "On what?"

"The time frame. Gary and I left the stage together." He looked toward the ceiling. "Let's see, she told us to take five and stormed off around midnight. I remember hearing the bells of Saint Cecilia's ringing the hour."

That jibed with what Justin Gambrell and Valentina had said. "So, you were together near midnight. Where did you go?"

He shrugged. "Nowhere in particular. As I said, there was no place open and, regardless, we were expected to reassemble in a few minutes. We strolled."

"Strolled?" A smirk was my answer. "Strolled where, for what purpose?"

"No reason, well Gary needed to calm down, and it was cool enough that I didn't fancy standing around, so I suggested a walk around the park."

"You mentioned your alibi depended on the time frame. Why? Did you part at some point?"

"Yes. I stopped to use the restroom and Gary was gone when I came out." He flashed a rueful smile. "I'm afraid I can't be sure of the time, though it was probably close to 12:30 a.m., or a little after."

Brianna was likely to have been murdered sometime after 12:30 a.m., which meant Gary did not have an alibi. I should have been pleased to have a solid suspect, but the thought of Gary being the killer gave me no pleasure.

I liked Gary Walston. If he'd committed murder, he deserved to be punished, but I wanted to be sure before I did something that would ruin his good name.

"He was gone when you finished in the restroom. But Gary didn't mention the two of you parting at any time. Did you meet up with him a few minutes later, perhaps?"

Roland shook his head. "Sorry, no. I didn't see him again until I went back to the stage. He returned a few minutes after I got there." He cocked his head to one side. "The only person I encountered after using the restroom was Valentina DeMarco."

"Valentina!" I frowned. "But she told me she was with Felicity Simms!"

Roland shrugged. "Not when I saw her."

If Valentina had been alone, and over by the restrooms, then neither she nor Felicity had an alibi. "If you don't mind, tell me what you saw."

He glanced at his watch and gave me a tight smile. "I'm afraid I'll have to leave after this, but it wasn't so much what I saw as what I heard."

"Heard?"

Roland nodded. "Yes. I'd just stepped out the door when I heard a noise followed by a woman's shriek. I started toward the sound when Valentina ran past. She was heading toward the river walk and her hand was pressed to her cheek."

"Her cheek? Why?"

"Well, my guess is someone slapped her face."

My eyes widened. "Why would you think that?"

"Because there were streaks in the blue paint on her face." One eyebrow rose as he looked at me. "You know she had her face painted like a peacock?"

I nodded, recalling how much I'd admired Valentina's face-painting skills.

Roland continued. "If I had to guess, I'd also say it was Brianna that did the slapping."

"Why would you think that?"

He smiled and rose from his chair. "Because Brianna came down the same path, a few seconds after Val ran past. Now, I really must go, does anything I've said help your case?"

I stood and rousted The Colonel. "Not sure, but it's interesting. I won't keep you, thank you for your time." I walked ahead of him out of the office but as I passed, Roland put his arm out.

"Wait, please."

Hands in his pockets, he cleared his throat and rocked on his heels, looking off into the distance. His apparent nervousness set alarm bells ringing in my head.

"I, um, thought you had to leave."

Roland nodded. "Yes, I do but ..." His gaze dropped to the floor and his voice was soft and hesitant as he continued. "I wanted to, that is ..." He sighed and looked up at me. "I wanted to ask you about those last moments of my son's life."

The air rushed out of my lungs. My heart started pounding and a fine tremor made my knees wobble. A million thoughts swirled around my brain, none of them useful, some inappropriate. I opted to be blunt, assuming that would shut down the uncomfortable conversation.

"I don't remember much of that night, and what I do doesn't make sense."

My answer made Roland straighten. He made eye contact with laser focus. "What doesn't make sense? Tell me what happened!"

Eyes wide, I stared at him in mounting horror. He wanted me to— I swallowed past the lump in my throat and fought against a rising panic. "I, I can't. It's ... I have ..." I swallowed again and bent to lay a trembling hand on The Colonel's fat head. After a few minutes with my buddy's comforting warmth, I was able to think more clearly.

Taking a deep breath, I rose and forced myself to look him in the eye. "It's difficult to talk about, Roland. I, um appreciate your need to—to have closure, but I'd suggest reading the official report."

He scowled. "Don't you think I have? That's why I have questions!" He dragged a hand through his hair and looked at his watch, muttering a few choice words. "I'm late. Look, can we meet and talk about this?"

"Roland, I don't think that's a good idea."

"Please, Holly! You said the report doesn't make sense and if we compare the oddities, perhaps we can—"

"You misunderstood! I said what I remember doesn't add up!" I gathered The Colonel's leash and stepped around Roland, heading for the door. "I can't help you, Roland. I'm sorry."

"Holly!"

The desperation in his tone made me stop on the threshold. Facing the door, I braced for what he might say.

"I'm taking a deposition in Charleston today, but I'll be dining at Mario's tomorrow at seven. Please join me."

If he'd been angry or accusatory I could have walked away with no compunction, but the parent in me responded to the agony and confusion in his voice before I could consider his request. "I'll ..." I sighed. "I'll try, Roland."

Chapter Eighteen

The meeting with Roland was a success, as far as my investigation went, but his parting request played like a broken record for the rest of the morning. I ran errands on autopilot and tried to ignore the need to make that decision by focusing on finding a killer.

According to Roland, Gary had not been with him during the crucial window when it was estimated that Brianna had met her grisly end. Roland had helped me confirm my number one suspect but having witnessed Valentina outside the restroom, he'd inadvertently provided me with two more options for the top spot on my list.

Roland had said Valentina was holding her cheek, and there were streaks in the paint on her face. As I stood in line at the bank, those lines on her face nagged at me. Tate had mentioned Brianna having something greasy and blue on her hand. Based on what Roland had witnessed, I suspected it was face paint, but I couldn't confirm that without speaking to Tate, and I'd been avoiding *him* because I still didn't know how to handle his New Year's Eve invitation.

Pulling out my cell phone, I entered all but the last digit of his phone number before chickening out; I'd run my relationship problem by Connie and then call.

Pushing the questions concerning Valentina to the back burner, I contemplated Felicity Simms. With her friend seen on the other side of the park, she was once again a viable candidate for the murder of Brianna Bellamy.

Motives vied for my attention. While I wouldn't discount it, hatred of the woman wasn't unique enough to rule anyone out. One way or another, Brianna had made enemies everywhere she went. I'd need to dig deeper to solve the case.

CAROLERS AND CORPSES

Business completed I tried to leave, but the teller offered The Colonel a biscuit followed by several people stopping us so that they could fuss over his royal pudginess. Ten minutes later, I finally exited the bank and made my way to Glitter and Garlands.

The craft store was bustling with customers. I jumped in and handled the cash register and soon enough the store was quiet, and Connie took a break.

"Thanks for the assist."

Connie put the "Closed for Lunch" sign up and we went next door to the CoaStyle office. We split the salad she'd ordered and settled at the coffee table.

I took a few bites of the walnut, apple, and arugula salad and then set down my fork in favor of looking over the suspect list we'd made.

"You any closer to getting Madison off the hook?"

"Maybe?" I stared at the list of names hoping for divine inspiration.

"Maybe?" Connie chuckled. "Not sounding too confident."

"That's because I'm not. Instead of eliminating people I've now got three top contenders."

Her eyes widened. "Who?"

"Gary Walston, Valentina DeMarco, and Felicity Simms."

"Seriously? I can't see any of them being a murderer."

"Neither can I, but they all have questionable alibis."

Connie nodded. "Okay, but why? Gary and Val are prominent businesspeople, and Felicity is a former teacher."

"True, but all of them were angry with Brianna."

Connie snorted. "Way I hear it, everybody was."

"You heard right!" I sighed and set the list aside. "Which is why I can't winnow it down to one person."

My friend finished off her lunch and grabbed the suspect list. "Okay, let's separate some wheat from chaff. You've talked to everyone on this list?"

"Yes, er no. I stopped by to speak with Kay Emory, but she'd taken a sleeping pill. I'll swing by tomorrow, but it's a formality."

Connie frowned. "Why do you say that?"

"Apart from her being less physically capable, I haven't uncovered any motive outside of the general dislike so many people felt for Brianna, and no physical evidence links her to the scene. That isn't true of the others."

"That's reasonable. Let's start with Gary. What are his motives and is there anything linking him to the crime?"

CAROLERS AND CORPSES

"His company is on the verge of bankruptcy, and he was counting on the Gray's Island Causeway construction project to pull himself out of the hole."

Connie whistled. "That'd do it, but why do you think he's hurting financially? I just saw some of his construction signs outside of the Surf and Turf restaurant. They're remodeling and adding on to the dining room."

I tipped my head to one side and considered what she'd said. "That's good news for him, but his foreman mentioned they were expecting layoffs, and when I went to Gary's home he had his boat and other equipment up for sale. He tried to tell me a story that he didn't use them anymore, but Gary is well known for his love of fishing."

Connie nodded. "Yeah, everyone knows if you can't find Gary he's probably on the water. Still, if that's all you have …"

"Nope. Madison went looking for her sewing bag that night and she said the lights were out near the craft tents. When Gary's foreman checked that string, he said one of the bulbs was loose and that if one bulb goes out, the whole section surrounding it will stop working."

I quirked a brow. "Gary would know that, and the alibi he claimed doesn't pan out. According to Roland Dupree, he stopped at the restroom a bit after midnight and when he finished, Gary was gone. He didn't see him again until everyone met up by the stage a little before one. That's enough time to loosen the bulb and murder Brianna."

Waiting until Connie had finished scribbling, I gave her my last reason to suspect Gary. "Next to the light pole, I also found a torn piece of paper. It turned out to be a gum wrapper for Clove gum." Connie glanced at me, brow furrowed. I explained. "Gary chews the Clove gum to help him stop smoking."

She sighed and made notes next to Gary's name. "I hate to think of Gary being desperate enough to kill, but you've made a strong case." Her smile was hesitant as she met my gaze. "So, you spoke to Roland?"

My friend meant well, but the sympathy and understanding shining in her eyes made my stomach roll and thinking of my meeting with Roland reminded me of the sword of Damocles hanging over my head. The less said about Roland the better. My reply was a noncommittal 'uh-huh,' but Connie took a leaf from The Colonel's notebook and dug in.

"How did that go?"

Ignoring her question or changing the subject came to mind but Connie was tenacious and I did need to make a decision. I grimaced and opened the can of worms. "About as expected. He wants to meet for dinner tomorrow night."

Connie's brows rose toward her hairline. "My goodness, whatever for?"

"He wants to know about the last minutes of Shawn's life."

"Oh my God! What did you say?"

"What could I say?" I rose and paced around the room. "I understand his request; I'd need to know if the situation was reversed. But ..."

"But? You didn't agree to meet, did you?"

"I said I'd think about it." I snorted and glanced at Connie. "Of course, now that's about all I *can* think about."

Connie frowned. "Don't do it. You owe him nothing. The shooting was justified."

"Was it though?"

"Holly! What kind of question is that?" She jumped up and blocked my path, forcing me to stop and meet her gaze. "You know you acted in self-defense and Roland does, too. The police report made that very clear."

She was right, but my gut, and the fragmented memories that plagued me, said otherwise. I shared my belief with Connie, but instead of a vociferous argument her expression turned thoughtful.

"What?" She started to speak and then shook her head. "Come on, you were going to say something."

She shrugged. "It's nothing." A pointed look from me made her huff. "Okay, I was just remembering what I found on Megan Hearn's flash drive. The one with future podcast ideas?"

My stomach muscles tightened as I remembered what Connie had found while helping me save Dewey from a murder charge. Local podcaster Megan Hearn had been planning to do a series about the shooting that took Shawn Dupree's life.

Since Hearn had specialized in cold cases, her notes on the incident had given me pause but in the busy weeks following the arrest of her killer, it'd slipped my mind.

I glanced at Connie. "You're thinking Hearn stumbled upon new information?"

She shrugged. "I don't know, but you seem to think something is fishy and Hearn was good at ferreting out secrets. I still have a copy of her files, want me to take another look?"

"You don't mind?"

"Heck no, but it'll probably be after Christmas."

CAROLERS AND CORPSES

"That's fine, I'm too busy to focus on it right now anyway, but I do think I'll meet with Roland."

Connie winced. "Sure that's a good idea? You haven't had an episode lately; won't it be risky bringing this all up again?"

Risky was an understatement. I hadn't had a waking flashback in weeks. Instead of full-on panic, talking about what I remembered of that night mainly caused me discomfort. I could take a bit of shaking and a queasy stomach—better than fainting any day.

It was trying to remember what occurred after I exited the squad car that sent me into a tailspin. The nightmare I'd had since running into Roland nagged at me. I mentioned that initial confrontation and the subsequent nightmares to Connie. She wanted me to avoid the entire subject, but burying my head in the sand had never been my style.

"Meeting Roland won't cause a panic attack. Even when I ran from him Sunday night it wasn't because of the trauma."

Connie frowned. "Then why did you scurry away like a frightened rabbit?"

Did I dare say it out loud? I'd sidestepped the question during therapy, but Connie wouldn't judge me. I drew a deep breath. "I ran because I realized I couldn't honestly say I was sorry for killing his son. I couldn't make myself pay lip service to manners when I don't feel guilty." I gulped and met my friend's gaze. "Makes me a horrible person, huh?"

Her eyes widened. "No! You aren't a murderer! You did it to save yourself! The kid drew his gun!"

And there it was, the thing that haunted me. I looked down at the floor, watching The Colonel's fat belly expand and contract in concert with his snores as I forced myself to talk about the nightmare. "Connie, I have no memory of Shawn pulling his gun."

She gasped and I met her gaze. "In fact, I don't recall any confrontation with him." A vision of me blinded by the pick up truck's headlights and confused about what was laying on the ground entered my mind. "I got out of the car with my gun drawn, but I don't know why."

I blinked and the image faded, replaced by Connie's worried face. "All I know is Shawn Dupree wasn't standing there waving a gun at me."

Our gazes locked for a second longer and then Connie glanced away, biting her lip. "Holly, memories are funny things, especially after what you've been through." She looked back at me. "I really think you should just avoid him and the whole topic."

"That's what Dr. Styles recommended."

"See? My advice has medical backing." She smiled and picked up her ink pen. "That's settled, let's get back to finding a murderer."

Her pen was poised over the paper, and she wore an expectant expression, so I refrained from further comment. Besides, I'd already made up my mind. If I wanted a decent night's sleep, I'd need to exorcise the ghosts and making amends with Roland seemed like a good first step.

But first, I needed to find Brianna Bellamy's killer. I tapped my fingernails on the glass table and gathered my thoughts. "You wrote down the evidence against Gary?"

Connie nodded. "Yep, you mentioned Valentina but haven't said why."

"She was in the clear until I talked to Roland." I relayed what Roland had seen outside the restroom. "Val claimed that she went to comfort Felicity on the river walk and neglected to mention taking a circuitous route, so that makes me question both her and Felicity's alibis. Add in the streaks in her face paint and Brianna seen walking away." I shrugged. "Tate found a greasy blue substance on Brianna's hand. He sent it to the lab but I'm thinking it was the paint Val used. I gotta call Tate to confirm my suspicion but, if I'm right ..."

"Okay, give him a call and we'll have that settled... what's that look for?"

I rolled my eyes and cursed under my breath. My friend was eagle eyed or I had a rotten poker face. There was no use in beating around the bush, I needed a solution.

I bit the bullet and plunged into the murky waters surrounding my relationship with Tate. "I'm avoiding him."

"Avoiding ... why would you ..." Her lips twisted into a sly smile. "A little bird told me Tate's received a coveted invitation to the Osprey Point New Year's Eve bash. Know anything about that?"

Leave it to Connie to knock a hole in one. I sighed and fessed up. "As it happens, I came in today for a little advice on that subject. How do I turn Tate down without wrecking everything?"

"Turn him—are you out of your mind? Everybody wants tickets to that shindig! Girl, I'm green with envy."

While I wasn't a social climber or even much for parties, I could admit that I didn't want to turn the invitation down. Good company, a beautiful resort, what was not to love?

"Uh, exactly. So, why are you looking to say no?"

CAROLERS AND CORPSES

"Connie, it requires an overnight stay." Her expression was dumbfounded. I stared at her for a few seconds until the realization dawned in her eyes.

"Ooooh, yeah, that might be a problem." She winked at me. "For you anyway."

Another eye roll from me and Connie huffed but got back to the matter at hand. "Okay, okay, you aren't ready to have a deeper relationship. I get it, but let's put our heads together and find a work around because you *cannot* turn down that date!"

We tossed around ideas. I was lukewarm about most of them, but the suggestion that Mama would like a mini vacation and I could share a room with her was my final straw. "No, under no circumstances!" I sighed. "I'll just have to tell him I have other commitments. Surely he'll understand that."

"Other commitments like what? It's the holidays, he knows you don't have any job deadlines. No, let's think about it a little longer."

A few minutes passed. Out of ideas, I stared at The Colonel, wishing I could sleep that soundly without a care in the world, but presumably, Connie was thinking. She typed on her phone and then looked at me and grinned.

"I've got it!"

A spark of hope sputtered to life inside me. "Please tell me it's a great idea."

She snorted and stuck her tongue out. "It's my idea, of course it's great!" When I didn't dignify a response, she rolled her eyes and continued. "What are you getting Tate for Christmas?"

"Oh, come on! With the holiday market and now Madison's case, I haven't even thought that far ahead."

"Perfect! Then we'll kill two birds with one stone."

"How is a Christmas gift for Tate going to help me avoid an awkward sleeping arrangement on Osprey Point?"

"Oh ye of little faith!" My tone hadn't disguised my skepticism. Connie smirked and spelled out her plan. "Buy Tate a weekend golf package as a Christmas gift. Book it for the New Year's Eve weekend and voilà, problem solved."

My mouth dropped open. It was a brilliant idea, until my brain caught up and started pointing out the flaws. "Yeah, but I've left it too late, they'll be booked—"

"Way ahead of you!" She handed me her phone. "They have a golf package with a king room overlooking the river, and there's a spa getaway deal for you. Go on, get out your credit card and sing my praises while you enter the numbers."

CAROLERS AND CORPSES

It was the best idea I was likely to get. "I gotta hand it to ya, this seems to be a great idea." I dug for my card and punched in the information, studiously ignoring my friend's smug grin. "Done! Now to solve the mystery of who killed Brianna Bellamy."

Connie cocked an eyebrow. "Well, don't look at me, one bright idea per day is my limit. Besides, you're the super sleuth. I'm sure you'll have it figured out by dinner time."

"From your lips to God's ear." I stared at the hotel confirmation email and wished for a similarly inspired solution for Madison's problem; however, twisting the facts of the case in every conceivable angle, I was still left scratching my head. If wishes were horses, beggars would ride.

Chapter Nineteen

With my relationship problem seemingly solved, I left Connie's with a slight spring in my step. I still needed to find a killer and pull Maddie's behind out of the fire, but now that I didn't need to avoid Tate, I could dive deeper into the case.

Setting The Colonel loose in the garden, I perched on the porch steps and dialed Tate's number.

"Finally! Was beginning to get a complex. I've called you at least three times since we went to dinner."

CAROLERS AND CORPSES

"Well, hello to you, too!" Sidestepping uncomfortable subjects was proving to be my forte.

Tate chuckled. "Hey Holly, you doin' all right? Not being held at gunpoint by a crazed murderer?"

"Never letting me live that down, huh? And yes, I'm fine, just busy. Did you finish your conference?"

"Walking to the parking lot now. I should be home in a few hours. Want to grab a late dinner?"

The creak of the screen door drew my attention. "Uh, hold on a sec, Tate. Hey Mama, I'm talking to Tate while The Colonel does his business. Did you need something?"

Mama shook her head. "Not as such. Just wondering if you're going to keep your tail home tonight. Haven't seen you all week."

A laugh from Tate made me smile. "You heard?"

"Yeah, guess that's my answer. You spend time with Ms. Effie and have dinner with me tomorrow."

"Eh, how about lunch?"

"Why, got a hot date?"

"Yes, but not for the reasons you're alluding to. I'm going to meet Roland Dupree at Mario's."

Tate sucked in a breath. "What? Have you lost your mind?"

Despite the trepidation I felt in meeting Roland, I laughed. "Probably. At least Connie thought so, but after we talked she agreed I should do it. He wants to find out what happened to his son, Tate."

A snort rattled the phone speaker, and I could imagine him rolling his eyes. "We know what happened. His entitled son took a shot at you, and you defended yourself. Play stupid games, win stupid prizes."

That was harsh, and I told him so.

"Truth often hurts. I strongly suggest you back out of this dinner, Holly." In the background, I could hear his turn signal and a distant car horn. After a minute, Tate started in on me again. "Sorry, had to merge onto the highway. As usual, Charleston traffic is a nightmare."

"Then you should hang up and concentrate. I just called to ask if you'd gotten the lab results on that greasy substance found on Brianna's hand."

"Oh ho, I see. Only call when I have something you want!"

His teasing indignation made me laugh. "Well, gotta make yourself useful to keep a gal."

A bark of laughter traveled down the line. "Cold, Holly Daye, harsh and cold. But such are the indignities a poor bachelor must suffer if he's to have a little comfort in his dotage." Tate continued as I tried to stifle my laughter. "As it happens, I did get the results back from the lab. Care to guess what the blue goo was?"

"I'm hoping it was face paint."

"Ha, got it on the first try. Good, old grease paint, otherwise known as theatrical makeup. How did you guess?"

I told him what Roland had witnessed.

"So, you think Valentina DeMarco is the killer?"

"Not exactly. There's more evidence pointing to Gary Walston, but Val is definitely a close second."

"What will you do now?"

Tate's question drew me up short. I'd been so focused on confirming my hunch I hadn't given much thought to the next move. "Not sure. I've talked to everyone on my list, well except for Kay Emory, but I'll run out and talk to her tomorrow. After that I'm fresh out of clues to follow."

"Does that mean you'll turn everything you've discovered over to the police?"

A snort was Tate's answer. He responded with a deprecating laugh. "What was I thinking? This traffic must be affecting my cognitive functions. Speaking of things are choking down again, I'd better go."

"Hold on Tate."

"Ah, what can this poor, beleaguered coroner do for you now?"

I grinned. "You can accept that Osprey Point invitation."

His exuberant response made me wince and pull the phone away from my ear. After he'd calmed down, I dropped my caveat. "On one condition."

"Oh man, here it comes. Hold on while I brace for impact."

"Stop it." I giggled. "I'm not making you take Mama or Dewey!" I ignored his muttered *thank God* and continued. "I'll go with you, but you have to leave the lodging arrangements to me, okay?"

He was silent so long I wondered if we'd lost the cellular connection. I was about to call his name when he cleared his throat. "I was going to make room reservations, but what do you have in mind?"

His wary tone made me chuckle. "Don't be so suspicious! It's a surprise and you'll love it."

"A surprise? Now I'm *really* worried."

"Deep breath, Tate. Surrender control, you'll feel better."

CAROLERS AND CORPSES

He laughed, made an off-color remark that I chose to ignore, and we said our goodbyes with a plan to meet for dinner the day after tomorrow.

Confirmation of my suspicions had left me in a quandary. I propped my chin in my hand and absently watched The Colonel scurry about the yard as I ran through my options now that I knew Valentina had been in contact with Brianna shortly before she died.

Gary still had the most evidence against him, but Val was a close second. I also couldn't discount Felicity since her alibi was tied to Valentina's. Regardless of evidence, I wasn't any closer to solving the mystery and no solution was jumping out at me.

Deciding the best course of action was to interview Kay and then turn all my findings over to Madison's attorney, I leaned back against the steps and let my mind drift to the coming dinner with Roland.

Despite my fear that delving into that fateful night might instigate a panic attack, I was committed to my course. My gut said something wasn't right. Whether it was distorted memories or a flawed police report was anyone's guess, but talking to Roland and hearing what was troubling him might spark my own memories or, at the very least, give me a new avenue to explore.

Aside from my concerns over Madison and Roland, I also had to face facts about my relationship with Brooks Junior. He'd rang while I was on the phone with Tate. Calling myself every sort of bad mother, I'd still chosen to ignore it but sooner rather than later I'd have to see what he'd wanted.

It was a week until Christmas and I still hadn't confirmed Junior's attendance at Myrtlewood; a fact Mama was none too pleased about.

A light breeze blew in over the river, making me shiver. I started to rise, when a flash of brown barreled out of the shrubs and crashed into my legs, almost tipping me back onto my behind.

"Boy! You're a tank." I patted The Colonel's back and grimaced. "Ugg, what have you been into? You are sopping wet!"

With a strong suspicion my dog had been chasing koi in the ornamental pond, I whistled for him to follow and made my way to the back porch and the utility sink. After a quick wash that left me bedraggled, I toweled The Colonel off and jumped into the shower. With any luck, my delay would earn me a night of peace. Surely Mama would be ready to retire by the time I finished.

CAROLERS AND CORPSES

To my dismay, Mama was bright-eyed, if not bushy-tailed, and, when I walked into the TV room I knew why. Perched on the edge of her recliner with a bowl of popcorn in her lap, Mama's attention was glued to the set while a montage video of Sanctuary Bay played and Grace Neely pontified in the background.

"Hey Mama, have you finished your shop —"

"Sssh, it's breaking news!"

My polite to a fault Mama had shushed me! I closed my gaping mouth and braced for the world to end. Awaiting my turn to speak, I flopped onto the sofa. The Colonel was snoring, but unfortunately it wasn't loud enough to drown out the nasally harpy spreading verbal manure on the television.

Waiting for Neely to pause for air, or station identification, I stared at the set, absently noting the crew had filmed outside the Split Bean as well as portions of the holiday market and river walk.

My eyelids were drooping, and I was about to bid my mother goodnight when an image on the screen jolted me awake. I stiffened and sat up straight as I watched Grace Neely standing beside our gated driveway come into focus.

"And finally, as if a former law enforcement officer inserting herself into an active murder investigation and attempting to subvert justice on behalf of a cold-blooded murderer weren't enough, sources tell me the detective working tirelessly to hold poor Brianna Bellamy's killer to account is being pressured to slow walk the investigation from someone higher in the chain of command." My fingers clenched into a fist as a smirk twisted Neely's perfectly painted lips. What I wouldn't give to wipe that smug look off her face!

"Ultimately, the DA will have to decide, but, considering new evidence that we aren't yet at liberty to reveal, it will be down to small-town corruption if Madison Ross isn't indicted by the end of this week."

My eyes widened. The nerve of that woman! I'd started listening late in her tall tale, but the implication seemed to be that, due to my family's long history in Noble County and my having served on the force, I was attempting to scuttle the investigation.

Gritting my teeth, I waited for a commercial and then pummeled Mama with questions. "What new evidence? Where did it come from? Did that woman mention us by name? Were you here when they filmed outside the gates?"

CAROLERS AND CORPSES

"Holly Marie, I didn't understand a word you just said!" Mama reached for the remote and the television went dark. Pursing her lips, she set her popcorn aside and glared at me. "Now then, what is so important that you have to interrupt my program?"

Slowly, I repeated my questions.

"You heard her, they can't tell us about the new evidence yet. But it must be something damning if Grace thinks it will lead to charges against Maddie." Mama wrung her hands. "You know that Grace was a famous prosecutor before she got her show."

I refrained from rolling my eyes. Mama took my silence for agreement.

"Oh, I pray she's wrong for Madison's sake, but it doesn't look good."

On that we agreed. I bid Mama goodnight and prodded The Colonel into movement. It seemed my plans for tomorrow had changed. According to Ms. Super-Former-Prosecutor Neely, I had an inside track with law enforcement, and it was time I used it.

First thing tomorrow I'd visit my old department and prod Craig into divulging the so-called new evidence.

Chapter Twenty

Timing my visit to the sheriff's office to coincide with the morning shift change, I found the summons and liens department quiet, and Craig hunched over his computer screen. Perfect!

"Hey, stranger, ready for Christmas?"

"Well, look what the cat dragged in!" Craig rose and gave me a one-armed hug. He resumed his seat and quirked a brow. "Have a seat and tell me why you're here because it definitely isn't to ask me about the holidays."

"So skeptical. Can't an old friend drop by—"

"No, you avoid this place like the plague." He leaned back in his chair and motioned with his hand. "Out with it, Daye."

Grinning, I rolled my eyes and plopped onto the chair opposite his desk. "Okay, you've twisted my arm." Casting a glance over my shoulder, I leaned forward and whispered. "I need to know what new evidence Brannon has on Madison."

Craig shook his head and began to type. "Shoulda known." He met my gaze and smirked as he turned his computer screen toward me. "You know I could lose my job for this."

I nodded. "I'll be quick."

"Five minutes." Craig rose and walked out the door. "Gotta take a leak."

Grabbing the mouse, I scrolled through the case notes. Halfway down the page I found what I was looking for—they'd obtained Madison's phone and text records. My eyes widened as I read the last conversation she'd had on Sunday night.

Snapping a photo of the log, I jumped up and raced out the door, nearly knocking Craig over. "Sorry, gotta run. Thanks! See y'all at Myrtlewood for Christmas Eve?"

"Yep. We'll be there. Stay out of trouble, Daye!"

"Always!" Craig's bark of laughter followed me out of the office.

The Colonel was all wiggles and accusing looks when I jumped into the Scout. I reached into the glove box and handed him a treat. "Sorry buddy, it was a flying visit."

My punishment for leaving him in the car was The Colonel snorting and drooling on my seat all the way to Myrtlewood.

I bounced down the plantation's long drive at breakneck speed as the case notes replayed in my head. Madison had some explaining to do.

Setting The Colonel free to roam, I banged on the front door.

"Holly! I wasn't expecting you—"

"We need to talk."

Madison's eyes grew round. She stepped back and I motioned for her to follow me into the front parlor. The tree Dewey and I had brought was now decked with hundreds of twinkling lights, ribbons, and bulbs. At any other time I'd have raved over her creation, but what I'd discovered had set my blood to boiling. I got straight to the point of my visit.

"You failed to mention that you'd planned to meet Brianna Sunday night at the park."

CAROLERS AND CORPSES

Madison gasped. "How did you—"

"Find out?" I pulled up the image I'd taken at the police station. "The same way the cops did. I'd like an explanation."

She gulped. "This looks bad, doesn't it?" I nodded. She drew a shaky hand through her hair and drew a deep breath. "It was Mama's ring; you remember she was taunting me with it that night?"

"Yes, what about it?"

"I wanted it back. When you sent me home, I tried to sleep. I dozed off at one point, but when I woke up the thought of that witch wearing my mother's ring wouldn't leave me." She shrugged. "I texted Brianna and asked her to give it back."

I snorted. Brianna Bellamy wasn't the type to do anything out of the goodness of her heart. "But she refused."

Madison gestured toward my phone. "You read her reply. We went back and forth a bit and finally, she agreed to return the ring if I'd sign over ownership of Daddy's house."

"I read that, but I don't understand. I thought your father left everything to her."

Maddie nodded. "He did, sort of. She has some money outright and is the executor of the rest. The house, some stocks, and other stuff are all in a trust. She can't touch them, but she gets the income off investments and can live in the house until she dies. Then it all comes to me."

"And Brianna wanted the house?"

"Yes, in exchange for Mama's ring."

I frowned. "Madison, that house is waterfront property. It's gotta be worth at least a million, maybe more. Why would you give that up for a piece of jewelry, even one that belonged to your mother?"

Tears welled in her eyes. "It was Mama's engagement ring, Holly! I couldn't stand for that horrible woman to have it." She ducked her head and muttered. "I will never understand why Daddy married her."

"I think she tricked him."

Madison frowned. "What? How?"

"She had a reputation for having affairs and then blackmailing the men. My guess is she told your dad she was pregnant."

Maddie sucked in a breath. "Oh my God, but why? And, if that's true, how was she going to explain when she didn't have a baby?"

I shook my head at Madison's naivety. It was both refreshing and worrisome. No one should be that trusting. "Your dad was a wealthy and influential man, Madison. For someone like Brianna he was a great catch. As for the lack of a baby …" I shrugged. "An older man like Clayton? He wouldn't have questioned her if she claimed to suffer a miscarriage."

"Oh, that's awful! Poor Daddy. She played on his honor."

"Yep. And rumor has it, she's done it before, but that's neither here nor there. Why didn't you tell me about this meeting? You look guilty."

"You think I killed her?"

"No, but this is damning evidence and it'll probably convince the DA to issue an arrest warrant."

She paled and started to tremble, but I was in no mood to offer comfort. She'd lied to me, even if by omission. "What happened when you met her?"

Madison shook her head and sniffed. "I didn't. Everything happened just as I said, except for why I went back there. I waited by the craft tent, but she didn't show."

"You didn't go looking for her?"

"No, I heard that weird noise and got scared," She shrugged. "I was walking back to the parking lot when Dewey stopped me and said I had to join the others by the Christmas tree. Will I go to prison, Holly?"

I sighed and got to my feet. "Not if I can help it."

She followed me to the truck. I was loading The Colonel into his seat when Madison touched my arm.

"I'm sorry I lied to you. I just thought you might not believe me if I told the truth."

"It's never a good idea to lie, Madison, and in this case, it makes you look guilty." Tears started to fall, and I relented. "Don't worry, I'm close to finding the killer."

She sniffed and hugged me before I got into the truck. The lecture I'd just given her played in my head as I watched her return to the house.

My assurances that the case was almost solved set a frisson of unease clawing at my spine. I needed to take a leaf out of my own book. It was never a good idea to lie.

After a stop for lunch, I made my way out to Gray's Island. What I'd told Madison wasn't an out-and-out lie, but with only

CAROLERS AND CORPSES

Kay Emory left to interview, there was a strong possibility I'd get my words thrown back in my face.

Gary Walston was still the most likely killer. I should have been driving to the sheriff's department and begging Joe Brannon to at least consider what I'd discovered before an arrest was made, but a job worth doing was worth doing right. Even though Kay was far down on my suspect list, I needed to talk to her before pulling the trigger on Gary.

The Emory's gate was open, and I spotted Kay as I pulled up to the house. She was making her way back to the house along the wooden path that gave them access to the beach. The Colonel was chomping at the bit to explore so I met Kay halfway.

Her wheelchair trudged at a snail's pace, the engine whining as it struggled to navigate the rough terrain. I raised my voice and called out a greeting. "Afternoon, Kay! Feeling better?"

She pulled alongside me and smiled. "Hey Holly! Yes, it's a glorious day. I'm sorry I missed you before. It was one of my bad days."

I waved away her apology. "It's fine, wasn't a wasted trip. I had a nice chat with your better half—Colonel, no!" Like the bull the breed derived their name from, The Colonel barreled up to Kay and jumped on her legs, leaving sandy pawmarks on her leggings.

"Oh Kay, I'm so sorry." Black with dancing gingerbread men scattered across the fabric, I recognized the artwork style as a prominent and expensive designer's work.

Gritting my teeth and praying I wouldn't have to shell out a couple hundred on new pants, I pushed The Colonel away and squatted to brush at the marks. "I think it will come out. These are so cute, too! I noticed you wearing them at the holiday market opening."

The paw marks disappeared with little effort but two lines of something white and chalky proved more stubborn. "Darn it, I'm sorry Kay but there is a line of something just below your knees that won't come off. It's on both legs, too." Frowning, I swiped at them again. "Whatever this is, it refuses to come out."

Kay leaned over and shook her head. "Oh, I don't know what that is, but The Colonel didn't cause it. I noticed them when I got home the other night." She sighed. "Won't even come out in the wash. That's why I'm wearing them around the house. Is it really noticeable? I'd hoped to keep them through the holidays."

Grateful that The Colonel had caused no lasting damage, I shook my head and attempted to rise. "Nah, from a distance

CAROLERS AND CORPSES

you can't tell—oh!" Never very agile, my injured leg had made matters worse and, if not for catching myself on the footrests of Kay's chair, I'd have ended up on my rearend.

Kay grinned. "Need help?"

I got a better grip on the sandy footrest and finally managed to get to my feet. "We're a pair, aren't we?"

Kay chuckled. "It's easy to forget our bodies don't work the way they used to." Her expression showed nothing but good humor in her situation.

Taking a leaf out of her book, I resolved to count my blessings every time I was tempted to curse my need for a cane; it could have been much worse. Swiping my hands together, I managed to get most of the grit off and followed Kay as she led the way back to the house.

After a brief stop by the back door so that Kay could take a broom to her feet and the wheels of her chair, we went inside. "Let's make tea and we'll have a nice chat."

We settled in her living room, quiet since her husband wasn't glued to the television. The room had been straightened since I'd last visited and along with the picture of her son winning the soccer award, there was a new image. I picked up the gilt frame and studied it.

"Oh, that's my sister and her husband at the opening night of his latest film. Isn't her dress divine?"

"Yes, she wears it well." A handsome couple were standing on the red carpet outside of a theater. Both were dressed to the nines and posing for the cameras. I set it aside and looked at Kay. "Is your sister an actress?"

Kay shook her head. "She's done a few small projects, but her husband is the star; he's directed all of those action movies, the ones with the fast cars and leggy blondes?"

Though I hadn't seen a Hollywood movie in a decade and had no clue what films she was referring to, I nodded. "That's cool. I had no idea your sister was in Hollywood. Don't know how she can stand it with all the gossip and stuff." I snorted. "Not that Sanctuary Bay is short in that department."

Kay laughed. "Oh, Zoe is usually the ringleader with that. As Derek's wife, she's got a lot of power behind the scenes." She gave a spiteful laugh. "As Brianna Bellamy found out!"

"What? Your sister knew Brianna?"

"Oh yes." Her expression morphed into one I was all too familiar with having spent a lifetime with a gossip-queen mother. Eyes bright, Kay leaned forward and smirked. "After my accident, Zoe flew in and stayed with me for a few months. While she was away, Brianna tried her tricks on Derek."

"Tricks?" I had an inkling as to what Kay was alluding to but wanted confirmation.

"You know, her innocent, helpless female act. She also tried it on Eugene Simms and it worked on Clayton Ross, the fool that he was. But, before she came to Gray's Island, Brianna attempted to seduce Derek. I don't know all the particulars, but when she couldn't lure him away from my sister, the witch tried to smear his name by spreading lies."

My eyes widened. Justin Gambrell had mentioned Brianna having to leave Hollywood. Was this the reason? "Did it work?"

Kay snorted. "Of course not! A friend called Zoe and she hightailed it back to California. Between her and her friends, the tables were turned on Brianna, and her name was mud. She couldn't have gotten a job to save her soul when Zoe finished with her. That's power!"

Indeed, it was. I knew all too well how destructive tongue wagging could be but, in Brianna's case I had a hard time sympathizing; she had been anything but a victim. Something nagged at me, but Kay changed the subject, and I lost the thought.

"I'm sorry Kay, I was woolgathering."

"Oh, I just asked how the investigation was going. I saw the news last night." Her mouth drooped. "They seem to believe Madison will be arrested soon."

Not if I could help it. But Kay's question gave me an opening to turn our conversation to the point. "You shouldn't believe everything they report, Kay. Everything they have on Maddie is circumstantial at best."

She tilted her head and cocked a brow. "You're still looking for the killer then?"

"Yep, and I've narrowed things down quite a bit. Speaking of suspects, you're the last person I need to interview." She stiffened and I rushed on. "Just a formality, Kay. I'm talking to everyone that was in the park after hours. I understand Brianna got into a scrap with Felicity Simms and then called for a break. Can you tell me what you did during that time?"

Kay's shoulders relaxed and she smiled. "Sure. I stayed at the stage, the sprinklers came on and made it difficult to navigate in my chair—oh, wait! I made a quick run to the restroom. There and back in about ten minutes. Does that help?"

I nodded. "Did anyone happen to see you?"

She laughed. "I need an alibi?"

"It'd help." I smiled to take the sting out of my words and Kay grinned.

"How exciting. This is like Perry Mason!" She tapped her finger against her bottom lip. "Now, let me think. Everyone took off and I was sitting there alone ... then Valentina ran by. I waved, but I don't think she saw me. It was just after she passed that I decided to attempt a call of nature. It was slow going though, should have seen the mud on my wheels!"

The Colonel was starting to fidget and sniff around; a sure sign he was looking for a place to potty. I rose and gave The Colonels leash a slight tug.

I'd never considered Kay a strong suspect and, if needed, I could verify her alibi with Valentina.

My dinner with Roland Dupree was weighing on me, and sipping tea with Kay Emory was only delaying the inevitable.

"Thanks for the tea and company, Kay. Time I headed back to Sanctuary Bay."

"Oh, must you go? It gets lonely out here alone all day." She followed me to the door.

"Sorry, I really have to go but we'll get together after the holidays." I smiled and shoved my stubborn bulldog out the door. "I'll bring Mama."

"Oh, that will be nice. Wish Ms. Effie a merry Christmas for me!"

"Will do." The Colonel dragged me down the sidewalk as Kay closed the door. He did his business, and we were on the road. Thoughts about meeting Roland ran through my head the entire way home.

He'd told me he wanted to know what his son's last moments were like. Could I talk about that at all? Even if I managed it, dead children was hardly a topic to aid digestion.

Chapter Twenty-One

Committed to joining Roland in just under two hours, I'd intended to take a hot bath and relax before walking into the lion's den. But my best intentions were stymied when Junior knocked on the front door a few minutes after I got home. I held the door for him, but he declined, claiming he couldn't stay.

Grabbing a sweater, I shooed The Colonel into the yard and joined my son on the porch swing. Since we hadn't managed more than three civil words in as many months, I remained silent, letting him take the lead.

Several uncomfortable minutes passed before Junior sighed and got to the point. He cleared his throat and nodded toward a pile of wrapped boxes sitting beside the door. "Thought I'd drop off y'alls gifts before I leave."

I frowned. "Leave? Christmas is next week, where are you going that you won't be able to give them to us at the proper time?"

Junior rolled his eyes. "Dad is taking Alexa and me to Colorado for the holidays."

"What? You aren't coming to Myrtlewood for Christmas?"

He cocked a brow and, by the look on his face, I assumed the answer to my question. I'd had another restless night, plagued by the now familiar nightmare interspersed with twisted images of Madison being sentenced to life in prison.

The weather had turned cold and damp, which made my leg ache like the devil, and now, because of my selfish ex-husband, Junior was planning to break a holiday tradition we'd observed without pause since his birth. Thirty years of tradition wrecked because Brooks Daye wanted to score points off me. I saw red.

CAROLERS AND CORPSES

"That jerk!" I leaped from the swing and started pacing, each step fueling my rage. "He knows how important the holidays are to Mama! Tradition is everything and she isn't getting any younger! He's just doing this to spite me and—"

"Mom ..."

"And he knows how much it'll hurt me if Mama's —"

"Mother!"

I jumped and turned to find Junior glaring at me. "What?"

Junior huffed. "Stop bashing Dad! This is why I don't come around! You always do this and I'm sick of it! He mentioned giving me a trip to Vale for a Christmas present because he knows how much I love to ski." I rolled my eyes and Junior scowled. "It was *my* idea to take the trip over Christmas and have him join us!"

"Your idea?" My anger was dissipating as the truth sank in. "But Brooks, you're breaking a family—"

"*Tradition.*" He sneered dragging the word out like it was something foul on his tongue. "Family! Spare me, we haven't been a family for years."

My eyes widened. "That's not true! I've tried to keep everything the same. Myrtlewood is decorated and ready for us to spend a few days relaxing and just being together. It's your father who ruins everything!"

"There you go again! Always blaming Dad. Every time I mention him you attack and cut him down."

"I do not!"

He snorted. "Yeah, you do Mom, or are you forgetting the dirty old man comments or filthy pervert?" He threw up his hands and turned on his heel. "You know what? I don't need this. Have a merry Christmas, I'm outta here."

Having my words thrown back at me hit hard. I gulped. "You're right, I have said some awful things, and I'm sorry."

Junior huffed. "Whatever, I gotta run."

"Brooks Wyatt Daye! I said I was sorry. What's gotten into you? I didn't raise you to be so rigid and unforgiving."

His shoulders stiffened and his lower lip jutted out. For a minute I thought he'd walk away but as suddenly as he'd puffed up he deflated with a sigh.

He nodded. "I'm ... uh, sorry. Whatever is – it's between you and Dad." He glanced at his phone. "I'm late—"

"Junior, wait!"

CAROLERS AND CORPSES

He paused, back ramrod straight, one foot on the step. Tension radiated from him, and any minute I expected him to stomp off and never speak to me again.

He'd always been closer to his father but the level of hostility my son had shown me since the divorce was unprecedented and, if left to fester, I feared he'd fade out of my life completely.

"Look, we need to talk."

He sighed, texted something, and then met my gaze. "I don't have long; I'm supposed to be meeting Alexa to shop for our trip."

Great, no pressure. I drew a deep breath and tried to calm my thoughts. The last thing either of us needed was another argument. I stared at my son and tried to figure out where everything had gone wrong. It had started just after his father announced he was leaving.

My divorce had been sudden, not unexpected per se because Brooks and I had drifted apart years ago. We'd each went our own way and managed to live in distant affability.

I'd tried several times to find common interests and relight whatever spark we'd lost but he hadn't seemed interested, and I just got on with things. Regardless, I'd fully expected to grow old with the man.

Then I'd been shot and nearly died. At the time, I was too busy fighting for my life, but apparently for Brooks, it put things into perspective. Life was short, too short to be with someone that you loved, but weren't *in* love with.

I'd been furious when Brooks had announced he was filing for divorce and rightly so. The timing couldn't have been worse, but with hindsight, I'd reached the same conclusion that Brooks had; life was indeed too short and there was no promise of tomorrow.

Our son was an adult. He had a fiancée, a law degree, and was a junior partner in his father's firm. Yet, I wondered if his hostility was stemming from the same place many younger children of divorced parents found themselves.

"It wasn't your fault." The words were out as I was still formulating the thought. Junior looked over his shoulder, brow furrowed.

"What?"

I tried to explain. "The divorce. What happened between your father and me had nothing to do with you."

His puzzled expression turned to exasperation. "I know that! Why would you think that I blamed myself?"

Shrugging, I walked across the porch and sat on the top step. "We've never talked about what happened." I glanced up and caught his eye. "The shooting, me nearly dying, your father leaving. All of our lives were upended, and well maybe you were angry and blamed me? Subconsciously anyway."

His eyes widened and he started to shake his head. "Like I said, it's none of my business—"

"Yes, it is Junior! You're a part of our relationship and deserve an explanation, especially now that you're engaged. Maybe, if you understand what went wrong for your father and me, you'll avoid the same mistakes." I'd expected him to argue but, to my surprise, he sighed and sat beside me though he avoided looking at me by staring out at the yard where The Colonel was happily digging to China.

Taking his silence for interest, I continued. "I grew up with two parents, grew old, and raised my own family seeing them remain in a stable relationship. I never dreamed it would be any different for you but, your dad and I ..." I sighed and acknowledged the truth.

"We were too young and got married for all the wrong reasons."

He glanced at me, a frown marring his handsome features. "What do you mean? I thought you guys were high school sweethearts."

Funny the things you assumed. I'd never made any secret about when Brooks and I had married, nor the date of Junior's birth, and yet, he'd apparently never done the math. I debated not dropping the penny but, after a few minutes of weighing the pros and cons, I filled him in.

"We did date all through school, but the reason we got married was, well I got pregnant, and our parents insisted."

"They made you marry because of me?"

I shrugged. "More Grandmother Daye than Mama, but neither of our parents were pleased, and I don't blame them. I certainly wouldn't have been jumping for joy if you'd come home at nineteen and told me your girlfriend was pregnant! But you, we loved you, Junior. Heck, we loved each other!"

He frowned. "Then, what happened?"

I sighed. "We grew apart. Your dad was in law school, then he was building his practice. I was raising you and then, when you started school, I went to the academy and became a deputy." I shrugged. "We were busy with life. Work, Brooks's practice, your school and sports activities ... but then you graduated, and we both drifted apart because you were the glue."

Junior's shoulders drooped and his voice was barely above a whisper when he muttered. "It was all my fault, I ruined y'alls lives."

"What? Don't talk nonsense!" I slid my arm around his waist and squeezed. "We'd talked about getting married, your arrival merely accelerated the timetable." I sighed. "I honestly thought you knew. I'd of never told you if I'd thought you would feel like this."

He huffed. "You just told me I was the reason you agreed to marry someone you didn't love! How did you think I'd feel?"

"Not love? Don't be silly. Brooks and I were madly in love, or we thought it was love anyway. Can you honestly look back at your childhood and think we weren't happy? All those vacations? Little league, fishing, beach combing? We were always doing something as a family, and we were happy!"

"I remember."

My son met my gaze and I saw the vulnerability in his eyes. I'd been right, even as an adult, he'd believed the divorce was related to him. "Good, and you'll do the same when you have kids."

He cleared his throat. "I just don't understand – why now? After thirty years!"

"That many years was probably part of the problem." Junior frowned and I tried to explain. "When we married, we had a lot in common, but we were teenagers, hadn't seen or done much, you know?"

"Yeah, I guess."

"It's why I don't think people should get married so young. You don't really know who you are or who you want to be until at least your late twenties. And Brooks and I, well we have different interests. He likes to play golf. I like nothing better than anchoring off the point and wetting a line. He's interested in shaping policy and having political power, and I can't be bothered. Well, unless they are tyrannical or corrupt." I snorted. "And we certainly differ in matters of intimate relationships because I wouldn't dream of dating someone younger than my—"

"Mother!"

"What?" I smirked. "I'm just saying!"

Junior rolled his eyes. "It was gross."

I hid my smile until he grinned, and soon we were laughing until tears ran down our cheeks.

CAROLERS AND CORPSES

Junior chuckled and swiped at his face. "What was he thinking?"

"Ah, don't be too hard on him. Midlife crisis is real."

"Yeah, but most guys just buy a sports car." He snorted. "At least he's not with her anymore. I was dreading him bringing her to my wedding."

"Oh, then she's not pregnant ..."

Junior's mouth pressed into a thin line. He shook his head. "I see the rumors got around."

"Well, I'd heard but, no matter. I'm glad she's not." Junior cocked his head and frowned, so I elaborated. "Your dad and I are in grandbaby territory now." I shuddered. "I couldn't imagine starting over."

"Ha, true. I don't know how that rumor got started. Dad only went out with her for a few months."

"Oh, she probably started —" My eyes widened as a thought occurred to me.

Junior cocked a brow. "What?"

"Nothing, only I was gonna say maybe the girl started the rumor. Like Brianna Bellamy did. It snagged her a wealthy husband."

He scrunched his nose. "Come on, Dad's not that much of a catch!"

The naivety of men, regardless of age, made me roll my eyes. "Yes he is, son. Your dad is a wealthy man, as much as Clayton Ross was, and a girl would be set for life." I chewed on my bottom lip and considered what I'd learned about Brianna.

She'd tried to seduce Eugene Simms until she discovered he wasn't as well off as Clayton Ross, and, with Eugene, she'd have to contend with a wife.

According to Kay Emory, Brianna's Hollywood career was in a tailspin because she'd tried the same stunt with a director while his wife was away, and I'd just learned that wife was Kay's sister.

But would Kay have killed for her sister? It didn't seem like enough motivation, but if I added in Brianna's stopping the causeway build... Kay had lost her son because of that faulty road. I glanced at Junior. Would I kill for my son?

Without hesitation, but not over a road.

"I can see wheels turning, what are you thinking about so hard?"

I blinked and met Junior's gaze. "Nothing. Thought maybe I'd figured out who killed Brianna Bellamy but no, that's not it."

Junior's phone chimed. "That's Alexa, I really need to—"

CAROLERS AND CORPSES

"Of course! You go. We'll talk when you get back."

He bit his lip. "About the trip. I can ask Dad to change the reservations."

"No! No son, you guys go and have a great time. We'll miss you, but there'll be other holidays."

"You sure? Grandma will be upset."

I snorted. "She'll get over it." I nudged him toward the sidewalk. "You're an adult and if that's how you want to spend Christmas, you should. Don't live your life putting your own wants at the back of the line."

He opened his mouth and started to say something and then shrugged. "If you're sure."

"Yes! Now go, you've kept Alexa waiting long enough. Can't have her getting mad and dumping you. I'm waiting for grandkids!"

He laughed and kissed my cheek. "Thanks Mom. Talk to you soon."

Whistling for The Colonel, I headed inside feeling better than I had in months. I didn't like being at odds with my son, and now that we'd cleared the air, I had no intention of letting it happen again.

RACHEL LYNNE

Mama wouldn't be happy about Junior's Christmas plans, but she'd still have a houseful. It'd have to be enough. The grandfather clock chimed, and I rushed upstairs. Time to meet Roland for dinner; my reckoning had arrived.

Chapter Twenty-Two

Mario's was packed and for just a moment I considered turning tail, but Roland caught my eye and waved, thus sealing my fate. I patted the floor next to my chair, settling The Colonel with his busy bone, and wondered what I was going to talk about.

Once again, Roland took the bit between his teeth and ran. Sparing me the need to make small talk.

"Thank you for coming, Holly. I took the liberty of ordering a large pizza but feel free to order anything you like."

Mario's was known for its wood-fired pizzas and, even if it weren't, I doubted I could eat; my stomach was rolling and the thought of food made me want to hurl. "That's fine, I'm not that hungry."

Roland nodded just as the waitress came to take my drink order. I sent her on her way with a request for sweet tea and then stared at the flames of the pizza oven and prayed for divine intervention.

The silence was tense and awkward for several minutes before Roland cleared his throat. "I appreciate how hard this must be for you."

"And you." His hesitancy helped me find my voice. I leaned across the table and made eye contact. "Roland, I don't understand why you're doing this. I can only imagine your pain, and, well, how can you not hate the sight of me?"

He snorted and leaned back in his chair, holding my gaze for a long minute before sighing. "I don't hate you, Holly. A reasonable person might say I should but …" He shook his head. "I've lost my only child. I've read the official report a hundred times. It tells me he died by your hand and that Shawn's actions precipitated the shooting. Only the more I read that report, the less I believe it."

My eyes widened. I stared at him, trying to put my feelings into words. In the end, I fell back on what Roland had said. "I feel the same way."

It was his turn to be surprised. "You do? I mean ... wow, I thought I was crazy."

That made me laugh out loud. "Well, under the circumstances, thinking like me shouldn't be taken as an indication of sanity."

My sarcasm broke the ice. Roland chuckled and said if we were headed to the looney bin, he couldn't ask for better company. We talked about local happenings until the pizza arrived. Halfway through our three-meat pizza, the conversation turned serious.

"What is it about the official report that you don't find credible?"

Setting down my fork, I considered his question while I sipped my tea. "I don't think it's any one thing or even anything tangible. It's more a feeling, I guess."

He frowned. "You make it sound like you don't have a clear picture of what happened."

I blinked. Between Mama and her gossip factory, I'd thought it was common knowledge that I couldn't remember the events of that night. "Um, I don't." His expression showed confusion, so I elaborated. "I've been diagnosed with PTSD and, since leaving the hospital, I've been in therapy."

"Oh, I didn't realize." His eyes narrowed as he searched my face. "PTSD. Are you okay talking about this? I wouldn't want you to relapse or anything."

"Um, I wouldn't say I'm okay, but I want to try and ... I don't know, figure out what is bothering me?" My hand trembled as I reached for my glass, and I questioned the wisdom of talking about the shooting. No way did I want to make the evening news by losing it in a public place.

"And what is it that troubles you?"

Where to start? There were so many things I found unsettling about the whole subject. A vision of me drawing my weapon and opening my door flashed through my head. I glanced at Roland. "Sure you wanna know?"

He nodded. "Absolutely, it's why I'm here."

I drew a deep breath. "Okay, well a big issue for me is that I don't recall shoot—er, firing my weapon." I ducked my head and watched Roland from beneath my lashes. I still couldn't believe he wanted me to discuss killing his son. If our positions had been reversed, the last thing I'd want to do was calmly eat dinner with the person that took my child's life.

Roland stiffened and sucked in a breath. For a moment I thought he'd abandon his quest for answers and stalk out, but another deep breath, a controlled release, and he nodded. "Right, let's start with that."

He assumed a detached manner all lawyers seemed to cultivate. I admired his control but was confused by the statement. "Uh, start? What are we starting?"

"An investigation."

My brows rose. "What? I don't understand, there was a thorough—"

"Was it though?" Roland leaned across the table. "Holly, there are a lot of inconsistencies about this, and the official narrative doesn't address them at all."

I frowned. "Like what? I can't find fault with what I've read." I shrugged. "I just know it *feels* off."

"That's understandable if you really can't recall what occurred, but the questions I have aren't based upon *feelings*. I deal in facts."

"I didn't say I can't remember, just that what I do remember leaves me confused."

Roland's brows rose. "I see. Can you tell me what you remember? Maybe together we can, I don't know, make some sense out of this mess."

He wanted me to recount what happened. Could I do it? Did I dare? I'd been very lucky in recent weeks but that didn't mean I was cured. Still, I had to try, if only for my own peace of mind.

I coughed and took a sip of tea. With my hand resting on The Colonel's warm body, I closed my eyes and forced the memories.

"I'm driving through the gates. I come to a fork in the road and don't know which way to turn." A shudder ran through me and everything within screamed stop, but I reminded myself that I'd managed to tell the same story to Dr. Styles. There was no reason to let fear overwhelm me now.

I tightened my grip on The Colonel and pushed ahead. "A shot rings out and I turn left." I glanced at Roland. "I figured the shot was y'all hunting."

Roland nodded. "A reasonable assumption. Are you up to continuing?"

"Yeah, just let me get a drink first." I gulped the sickly-sweet brew and tried to find words to describe what I felt. "There was a pickup in the road, I came up on it not long after I turned to follow the shot."

Roland's brows rose. "A truck? What kind? What color was it?"

"Um, I don't know, the high beams were blinding me. Is it important?"

"I think it might be."

I sighed. "Okay, let me think." I closed my eyes and pushed the memory forward. For a minute, all I could see were halos of light so, I thought back to before I saw the truck. "I was coming out of the curve, ah, I got a glimpse of the truck before I was facing it head on. Don't know what make or model, but it was dark, maybe black or dark green? Charcoal, even. Does that help?"

"Indeed, it does." He watched me for a few seconds. "Holly, no one in my family owns a truck of those colors. The only truck we own is a beater we use at the camp and it's red, or was. Mostly primer now."

I bit my lip. "Okay, but how is that significant?"

"Whose truck was it? No one was supposed to be at the camp that weekend, certainly not Shawn. I struggle with all of this because no one can tell me why my son was where he wasn't supposed to be!"

My heart broke for him. I could only imagine losing a child, much less losing one to violence. "Roland, people change plans all the time. Maybe it was a friend's truck?"

His jaw tightened. "No, Shawn's best friend was getting married. That weekend was the bachelor party. He wasn't going hunting, Holly."

If that were true, I could see Roland's point; his son wasn't likely to skip such an important event, especially to go hunting. I said as much, and Roland nodded.

"Exactly, he wouldn't have missed the party, he'd been in on the planning of it! And another thing,"—Roland fiddled with the condensation on his glass—"we'd held a big hunt just after Thanksgiving and culled about ten deer. There were no plans to take any more for at least a year, maybe longer. We wanted to build the herd. Shawn knew that. The next time we were planning to hunt was in the spring—turkey season."

"I see." Though I really didn't. What did it matter about the herd or hunting seasons? Roland claimed to deal in facts, and the fact was, Shawn had been there that night, pulled his gun, and gotten himself killed.

"Roland, where are you going with all of this? What's the point?"

He scowled. "Point? Isn't it obvious? That report is wrong, they've ignored evidence and not addressed inconsistencies."

"People make mistakes, Roland. And, as I said, just because Shawn didn't tell you, doesn't mean he didn't change his mind. Maybe he just stopped by for something on his way to the party."

"Okay, then why were you there? Why look for Shawn at the hunting camp?"

My brows rose. It was a question I hadn't expected. "I was serving papers that day and Shawn's file slipped between the seats. I found it on my way home. I can't remember if I'd heard Shawn was out there or if I went because I was passing the camp entrance and saw the gates open." I shrugged.

He frowned and leaned forward; an intent look in his eyes. "The gates were opened, you're sure?"

"Um, yeah. How else would I have gotten in?"

Tension surrounded us as Roland descended into a morose silence. The Colonel sighed and stood up, a sure sign he was ready to go. I was, too.

I rose and gathered my things. "Roland, it's getting late and I think we've said more than enough."

His eyes narrowed and I thought he'd argue but, after a moment, he nodded and threw some money on the table. "Come on, I'll walk you to your car."

The last thing I wanted was more of his company but short of being rude, I was stuck. We walked down Bay Street in silence until we arrived at the Scout.

Unlocking the door, I boosted The Colonel into the passenger seat and made my way around. Roland held the door for me.

"Holly, I ... thank you for meeting with me. I understand it was difficult for you to talk about this, and well, I appreciate it."

I climbed into the truck and cranked the engine before meeting his gaze. "You're welcome, Roland. It must be just as bad for you, if not more. I'm just sorry I couldn't have been of more help. I'm just not sure what it is you're looking for ..."

He gritted his teeth. "I want to know why my son was out there! I want to know whose truck you saw, and frankly, I want to know why you shot him. Shawn was many things, not all of them good. But he would never have pulled his gun on you unprovoked, Holly."

My mouth dropped open. "Are you suggesting I've lied?"

CAROLERS AND CORPSES

His eyes widened. "What? No, of course not!" He sighed and rubbed the back of his neck. "I don't know what I'm saying. I just know the police investigation doesn't add up and … I thought you could give me some answers."

He stepped back and I closed the door, rolling down the window so I could respond. "I'm sorry, truly. If I think of anything, if more of my memory returns … but Roland, I've been told that I might never get total recall back, and well I have accepted that. Maybe you should, too."

When he glanced at me, his eyes were blazing. "Accept? Never! You can give up but I never will. I will find out why my son was killed or die trying!"

Roland's parting words rattled around in my head all night, and as I'd feared, I was haunted by more nightmares. The sun was breaking the horizon before my body told my overwrought brain to zip it and I fell into a deep sleep.

It was after two when I awoke, grouchy and out of sorts. The Colonel was still sleeping so I lay in bed, once again thinking of all that had occurred the night before.

Roland's insistence that his son being at the hunting camp was indicative of something sinister had unsettled me. If I were honest, it was because I agreed. The dream I'd had since first running into Roland diverged from my usual flashbacks in one regard; the time directly after I was shot.

What was it I'd seen after I fell to the ground? Everything about the dream shook me but it was the final seconds that sent terror coursing through me and caused me to awaken screaming and covered in sweat. Frustrated, I closed my eyes and forced myself to face the fear.

The headlights are blinding but something darts in the shadows to the right of the truck. I slide my weapon from its holster and open the door … I opened my eyes and frowned. What had I seen that made me pull my weapon?

That was the sticking point for me. With or without an official report, I *knew* I'd pulled my gun and that wasn't something I had ever done lightly. Whatever I'd seen that night had been the catalyst for everything that followed. I needed to know what had prodded me to reach for my gun.

A door slammed downstairs, breaking my concentration. I scowled and closed my eyes again, but seconds later loud voices roused The Colonel, and I gave up.

It was past time I got out of bed anyway. It was the last day of the fair. I had a million things to do before the bonfire was lit and, to top it all off, I still hadn't figured out who had killed Brianna Bellamy!

Dwelling on the shooting and Roland's obsessions were a luxury I couldn't afford; it was time to focus. Determined to get my mental house in order, I was about to practice my DBT therapy when another shout rang out. I sighed and headed downstairs.

The Colonel galloped ahead, and I found him barking and scrabbling at the laundry room door. I shooed him through the doggy door and entered the room.

I could hear Dewey raising cane and Mama fussing. I pushed the door open and frowned. Standing in his boxers and shirt tails, my brother was waving a pair of pants around and glaring at Mama.

"What is going on in here? Y'all are loud enough to wake the dead."

Dewey turned his glare on me. "Well, look who decided to grace us with her presence. Must be nice to lay about, but some of us have to work." He returned to shaking his pants at Mama. "And I can't do that with ruined pants!"

"Now Dewey, I washed them like I always do!" Mama wrung her hands. "I'll do it again if you like but—"

"I ain't got time, Mama! It's almost three and I gotta be there before the gates open!" He tossed his uniform pants on top of the dryer and started rummaging through the cabinet above the washer. "Ain't we got some kinda stain remover?"

"Here, you're making a mess." Mama nudged Dewey aside and handed him a spray bottle "I don't know what you think will happen though, I've already used this twice. Whatever you got into isn't coming out."

Dewey grabbed the bottle and started squirting liquid on the lower half of his pants. "I didn't get into anything! It's that old washer machine what done it! Or you put somethin' in with the—"

"Dewey, listen to Mama." Their bickering was giving me a headache. "If she says it's not coming out then you'll just have to wear them like that until you can buy a —"

"Look at 'em, Holly! I can't go out like this!"

CAROLERS AND CORPSES

I glanced in the direction he'd pointed and frowned. There was a chalky white line, just below the knee on both pant legs. "If you want to keep your job then you'll have to!"

I looked again as Dewey muttered something about buying new pants. The lines were faint against the khaki color, but still noticeable. It was odd, the lines were perfectly even across the fabric. What on earth could Dewey have gotten into?

"Dewey, how did you manage—" I'd seen those marks before, but where, what had I been doing?

"Oh, you menace! Holly, you've got to train that dog to stop jumping, just look what he's done to my clothes!"

I turned around in time to see The Colonel's muddy feet hit the floor. I was scolding him as Mama fussed and swiped at her legs. A light bulb went off. "The snow!"

Mama and Dewey stared at me like I'd lost my mind. "What?"

"Holly, that ain't snow! Dern dog has been in the garden—"

"Not that, Dewey, think! Your pants. You stood in the fake snow the night we found Brianna Bellamy. That's what caused the stain, and, if I'm right, it stained Kay Emory's leggings as well!"

Mama and Dewey started jabbering, arguing, and tossing questions at me. I ignored them and raced upstairs, The Colonel hot on my heels. Once in the quiet of my room, I pondered my revelation.

The Colonel's jumping on Mama had sparked my memory. He'd done the same to Kay, and when I'd attempted to brush away the sand, I'd noticed the marks on her pants; they were the same as the ones that marred Dewey's.

Since Dewey's ruined pants were the result of him standing knee deep in a faux snow drift, it stood to reason that Kay had done something similar. But that left me with a problem. Kay was confined to a wheelchair.

The run up the stairs was the final straw for my overworked leg. I flopped on the bed and began the stretching exercises that Lance prescribed as I addressed the question. Could Kay walk or at least stand for any length of time?

The PT routine reminded me of my last visit to the gym. When Lance had lectured me about maintaining concentration to avoid injury, he'd used Kay as an example of what not to do.

According to him, Kay had been making progress and should have achieved some level of mobility had she continued the sessions.

What if Kay had? The gym visits kept me on track and a few of the machines contributed to my continued healing but, if I were to stop and only do the exercises that didn't require them, would my leg continue to improve?

My guess was yes, and it was likely the same for Kay. If Brianna had been drugged, it wouldn't have required as much physical effort.

Assuming that Kay was able to walk or stand meant she was a stronger candidate for the murder of Brianna Bellamy, but what else did I have to link her to the crime? Gary Walston was still higher on my list because of the physical evidence and motive—money, or lack thereof, was a powerful motivator.

Aside from the fact that Kay Emory took powerful sleeping pills and might have somehow slipped them to Brianna, I didn't have any hard evidence, and I questioned the likelihood that mild mannered Kay could be provoked to commit such a vicious crime.

The only thing that came to mind was the fact that Brianna had tried to seduce and blackmail Kay's brother-in-law. Bad, but enough to goad Kay into shoving expandable powder down Brianna's gullet? I didn't think so, which meant I was back to Gary and possibly Valentina, based on her wobbly alibi.

Stretches done, I decided to let my leg rest until it was time to head for the holiday market. Tonight's bonfire was the culmination of all our hard work, and I wanted to be at my best. Staring at the ceiling grew old. I pushed myself up to lean against the headboard and spotted the blue journal used to record my DBT therapy. Perfect, I could settle my mind while my body did the same.

I glanced around the room, trying to decide on an object to guide my focus therapy. A hairbrush, bottle of perfume, and The Colonel's sweater had all been used before.

I looked at my nightstand and finding nothing interesting, I moved on to the dresser situated on the far side of the room and spotted the whistle I'd found.

Rolling my eyes in exasperation that I still hadn't turned that in to lost and found, I moved on to a gold framed picture of Junior. The picture of him in his soccer uniform made me smile.

At five, he'd been so cute in his uniform and watching a bunch of little kids scramble around the field like chickens with their heads cut off had been a riot. I couldn't wait for the day he had a son to follow in his footsteps.

DBT therapy required an object that held no emotional value, so I dismissed the photo and continued my search. My eye was drawn back to the whistle. Had I seen that somewhere?

CAROLERS AND CORPSES

My eyes narrowed as I tried to recall. I shrugged and stared at the photo of Junior, still worrying over the puzzle of the whistle. Oh! I was an idiot! Aaron Emory. That's where I'd seen the thing before!

Kay Emory's son had been wearing a whistle in his soccer photo, it was his award for being best referee of the year!

But how could I be sure the whistle I'd found had belonged to Aaron? If I could prove that ... I'd found it by the restrooms opposite to were Brianna had been killed.

Found beneath the dripping *hose* mounted on the side of the restroom to be precise. From the beginning, I'd thought the leaky hose had been used to activate the expandable powder that had choked Brianna Bellamy, and if true, it was logical to assume the killer had dropped it.

The only person that would have had Aaron Emory's whistle *and* been inside the closed park was Kay Emory.

As physical evidence went, it was good. But it could have been dropped at an earlier time, *and* I wasn't even sure they were the same whistle.

Things were adding up, but I needed to be sure. An accusation like that could ruin a person's life. Madison was a perfect example.

Absently staring at the whistle, I mulled over the case. Everything I had could be dismissed as circumstantial. Gary could have done it, Valentina and Felicity as well.

Then there was Kay. If I knew she could walk and that the whistle had belonged to her son, she'd go to the top of my list—but how to find out? I stared at the whistle and the answer presented itself on a silver platter, or in this case, a silver whistle.

Pocketing the whistle, I hustled The Colonel into the truck and made my way to Goodwin Park. With a little luck, I might just catch a killer.

Chapter Twenty-Three

Lines were forming at the gates when I pulled into the lot, and I could just make out a splash of red at the back of the park. The fire department would be kicking things off in under an hour.

Last minute issues with Pastor Duke's concession stand needing another extension cord and the musician scheduled to host the *Name That Tune* game being late diverted me from my mission, but a few minutes after the bonfire was set ablaze, I was back on course.

We'd set up a lost and found shelf in the concession building used during sporting events. Located far from the crowded bonfire area, it was the perfect place to lay my trap.

The cinderblock building was dark, damp, and musty. I searched the wall just inside the door and located the light switch but the bulb was dim, so I opened the roll up window enough to light my way and soon found the shelf we'd designated for lost items.

The holiday market had only been open for a week, yet the shelf was loaded with objects big and small. I stood on tiptoes and felt around for an empty space, finally finding room for the whistle in front of a stack of ball caps. I stepped back to assess and decided to perch the whistle on the edge and let the chain dangle; I wanted it to be easily found.

Satisfied I'd set the stage, I pulled The Colonel away from the grill he'd been avidly sniffing and made my way back to the bonfire, composing an announcement as I walked.

I'd get the entertainer to make a public service announcement mentioning lost and found and see if anyone's cage was rattled.

CAROLERS AND CORPSES

The only flaw in my plan was what to do if Kay showed up. I had no power to arrest or even detain her. I bit my lip and considered the problem until I entered the bonfire area and spotted the bright auburn curls of socialite Marla Cassidy. Where Marla went, Craig Everette, my best friend and active-duty cop, was sure to follow.

I joined Craig as he made his way back from the hot cocoa stand. "Hey man, got a minute?"

Craig gave me a suspicious, side-eyed look and kept walking. "For you? Not sure. Got my butt chewed over accessing that file, Daye."

Unrepentant, I grinned. "But you didn't lose your job."

He scowled at me and handed Marla a steaming mug of cocoa. "Go away, I'm relaxing and enjoying the music."

"Didn't realize you were into show tunes." I schooled my features and lamented. "Must be old age creeping in. Sad how it changes a man."

Marla laughed and Craig rolled his eyes. "You're a pest."

"But you love me, which is why you are going to do me a favor."

Craig snorted. "Oh yeah, like what?"

"Help me catch a killer!" I left him standing slack jawed and ambled up to the stage. When the singer finished, I begged for a moment of his time and instructed him on what to say.

Craig stopped me as I walked to the back of the audience. "What are you up to, Holly?"

I'd caught his attention and he was all business. I held up my finger and nodded toward the stage. "Listen."

A flourish of guitar chords, imitating a drum roll, rang out. "Hey, ladies and gents, some of y'all are careless with your things. A silver whistle on a chain was turned in to the lost and found. If it's yours, head on over to the sports field concession stand right away because this is the last night of the holiday market. No telling what will happen to it once they clear the park."

"Perfect, now we watch and wait!"

I scanned the crowd but didn't see Kay or anyone else reacting to the announcement, but I knew she was on the premises, I'd seen her van when I parked the truck.

"What's perfect? And what are we waiting for?"

Filling Craig in on my discovery and plan to catch Brianna's killer, he was quick to point out the fly in my ointment. "If she isn't in that crowd, how do you know she heard the announcement?"

CAROLERS AND CORPSES

He had a point. The musician's sound equipment only reached the immediate area. I frowned and mulled over the problem. "No problem. You stay here and watch for Kay; I'll go to the first aid station and make the announcement again over the PA system." I started across the field as Craig rattled off questions.

"What? Holly, wait a second. You can't go over there alone, what if she shows up?"

"It'll be fine." I half turned and smiled. "Wait about ten minutes and if she doesn't come out of that crowd join me at the sports concession."

Craig continued to protest but I dismissed him and hurried to make another announcement. Once that was done, I coaxed The Colonel into a trot and hightailed it to the ball field as fast as my gimpy leg allowed.

Finding a place of concealment on a park bench with a clear view of the concession booth, I settled in to wait; it didn't take long. I heard Kay before she came into view. The motorized wheelchair made a high, whirring noise reminiscent of a golf cart and another clue clicked into place and nailed Kay's coffin; Madison had mentioned hearing an odd sound when she went to meet Brianna.

There was no furtiveness in Kay's actions, telling me she had no idea the jig was up. She rolled past my hiding place and made a beeline for the booth. I let about five minutes pass and followed, watching for Craig as I crossed the field.

The minutes ticked by with no sign of him. It wouldn't take long for Kay to find the whistle. If she did that without being caught and coaxed into confessing, I'd be up a creek without a paddle.

"Come on, buddy. Time to catch us a killer."

Turning my cellphone's voice recorder on, I put it in my pocket and stepped across the threshold. The Colonel and I were just in time to catch Kay standing on her tiptoes to reach the whistle, just as I had earlier.

"Miracle of Christmas, Kay?"

"Holly! You startled me." Kay jumped and the whistle fell to the floor. The Colonel scrambled toward it, tugging his leash from my hand. Since he couldn't get past me, I let him wander the room and focused my attention on Kay Emory.

She frowned, shooed my dog away, and picked up the whistle. "Shouldn't you be at the bonfire, Holly?"

I shrugged and leaned against the door jamb. "I take it that whistle belongs to you?"

CAROLERS AND CORPSES

Kay's smile was strained as she nodded. "Yes, it was my son's. I'm so grateful someone turned it in." She gave a nervous laugh. "Can't think how I lost it. I always wear it around my neck."

I nodded and looked at her face. "Maybe it came off while you were struggling to force faux snow powder down Brianna's throat."

"What? I don't know what –"

"Or maybe that just loosened the chain and it fell off when you bent to turn the hose on." I continued talking as if she hadn't responded. "Since that's where I found it."

Kay stiffened as my words hit home. Her eyes narrowed. "What are you implying?"

I snorted. "Not implying anything, I'm stating a fact. You killed Brianna Bellamy."

"How dare you?" Her eyes went round as she breathed in through her nose. "What on earth would give you a reason to make such an absurd accusation?"

"Absurd?" I shook my head. "Now that I know you aren't confined to that chair, lots of things make sense."

She scoffed. "Like what?"

"For starters, I tripped over muddy ruts by her body; they match the width of your chair's wheels." A noise behind Kay drew my attention. The Colonel was back to licking the front of the grill. I rolled my eyes. At least it'd keep him out of trouble.

"Ruts? That's what you're basing this horrible accusation on?" She laughed, but it seemed forced.

"Aside from the ruts and the whistle, there's also the holes in the snow drift. They were clearly made by someone standing by Brianna's head."

Kay scoffed. "Well, those could have been made by anyone!"

"Maybe, but whoever left them would have permanent white stains on their pant legs." I stared at her. "Kinda like the ones that ruined your Christmas leggings. You know, the ones you admitted to wearing on opening night? The stains I tried to brush away along with the sand from The Colonel's paws when he jumped on you?"

The look in her eyes hardened. "You call that proof?" She snorted. "Good thing you retired, Holly. You'd make a terrible detective."

"Irrelevant, since I was never in that position. But, if it makes you feel any better, I have more." When she didn't respond I elaborated. I wanted to keep her occupied until Craig arrived. I had no idea how to stop her if she chose to leave. There was also

CAROLERS AND CORPSES

the fact that Kay hadn't confessed, and, despite my bravado, I doubted anything I'd found would lead to a conviction.

"Your chair left tracks by the body, your pants prove you were standing by the body, and your necklace was under the spigot. We can add the fact that you clearly have use of your legs." I looked at her chair, parked by the door and then back at Kay, standing across the room underneath the shelf. "And, you don't have an alibi for the time in question. Oh, and your chair was heard near the crime scene."

Kay shrugged. "Why would I kill Brianna Bellamy? I didn't like her, but then very few people did." She looked at her nails and faked a yawn. "Frankly, Holly, I couldn't have cared less about the little witch."

"Really Kay? Brianna Bellamy used her husband's influence to stop the Gray's Island Causeway construction. You are the main fundraiser for that project. In fact, you are passionate about it and that is because its faulty construction contributed to the accident that caused you to lose the use of your legs, if only temporarily, but more importantly, that road took your son's life." I cocked my head and quirked a brow. "Are you really going to stand there and tell me you weren't affected by Brianna's actions? That you weren't infuriated enough to kill her over it?"

Her face turned a mottled red and for several seconds her lips moved without making a sound. I jumped when she erupted.

"Yes, I hated that woman! With every fiber of my being, I loathed her. She caused *nothing* but trouble wherever she went! I should get a medal for putting her out of everyone's misery!" Her rage spilled over, propelling her body into frenetic motion. I took a step back as her pacing brought her closer to the door.

"That night, she was at her worst. Kept us all waiting for over an hour, then sashayed in like she was a queen and started barking orders!"

Kay stalked toward the back wall, and I relaxed slightly. I'd pushed her into confessing, but I wouldn't be at ease until Craig arrived. I snuck a glance out the serving window, but nothing indicated help had arrived.

"Felicity was a star." My attention returned to Kay as she rambled on. "You should have seen her, Holly. Stood toe to toe with that hussy and gave as good as she got. I was exhilarated seeing the little madam get a taste of what she so often dished out."

"Is that why you snapped? Because Felicity's argument got you hyped up?"

"No," Kay rolled her eyes. "And I didn't snap. I'd already killed her by that point."

"What?" I frowned and replayed what she had said. Was Kay losing her mind? The altercation with Felicity Simms had occurred *before* Brianna died. I corrected Kay and she laughed.

"Oh, you're right, technically she was still alive but …" Kay giggled, and gooseflesh appeared on my arms. "It was just a matter of time." Her lips formed a sly smile. "Elavil takes a few minutes to get into your system, but when it does? Pow lights out. And I'd given that tramp enough to knock out an elephant!"

My mouth dropped open. I'd suspected Brianna was drugged by Kay, but I'd figured it was a spur of the moment decision. "How Kay? How did you give her the drugs?"

She grinned and nodded toward her wheelchair. "I never leave home without my thermos and Brianna was a drinker; I knew she wouldn't turn down the offer of mulled wine, especially on a cold night."

Wow, I'd underestimated the level of Kay's fury. I shook my head. "As a mother, I understand your anger and frustration over Brianna scuttling the causeway project, but Kay, why go to such lengths? Why kill her? You'll spend the rest of your life in prison! How can the loss of your freedom be worth it?"

She laughed and spun around to meet my gaze. "Spend my life in prison?" She sneered. "I don't think so. With Aaron gone, there's nothing keeping me here." She slipped the whistle into her pocket. "Think I'll go somewhere warm. Bali? Nooo, the Maldives! My sister honeymooned there, and I've always wanted to go." Kay started for the door, and I leaped in front of it, pulling her wheelchair along to block her exit.

She snorted. "Out of my way, Holly."

"You're not going anywhere, Kay." I glanced out the window. Where was Craig? If she forced the issue, I had no way to prevent it. I spotted a baseball bat leaning against a storage bin. It'd have to do. "Stay back, Kay, I won't let you leave. The police will be here any minute."

Kay glanced at the bat in my hand and smirked. "That the way you want to play this?" She turned to her left and I noticed the bin full of baseball bats.

My mouth went dry as she chose a metal one and tested the weight of it in her hands. "There's one benefit to being confined to a wheelchair, even temporarily; it helps build your upper arms." She flexed her biceps before casually walking toward the kitchen area.

The Colonel, unaware of the world around him, was happily sniffing, snorting, and licking his way around the food preparation equipment. I sucked in a breath as Kay closed in on him and swung the bat, missing his fat head by inches.

"Did you know I was a home run queen on the high school softball team? Next time, I won't miss."

"Kay, please." My voice broke on a sob. There was no way I could reach my baby in time.

"Step away from the door, Holly, and this all ends. You and the bulldog go your way, I go mine."

"I ... Kay this isn't like you! You have three dogs and a cat! You volunteer at the animal rescue ..." She planted her feet and raised the bat. "You've fundraised for the shelter, Kay ... please. No!"

It all happened so fast. Kay looked over at me, a sneer marring her face and a cold look in her eyes. Without a doubt, she was going to bludgeon my innocent bulldog.

Holding my bat like a club, I ran, reaching Kay as the metal bat was coming around.

Strengthened by my fear, I brought my bat down, catching Kay on the forearm. A sickening crack reverberated off the block walls, followed by Kay's screams. Her weapon clattered to the floor as the door burst open. Craig rushed in, followed by two uniformed officers.

Ignoring Kay's cries for help, I scrambled toward The Colonel, hugging his oblivious self for dear life as the police did their jobs.

I rested my head on his back, letting the calm beat of his heart soothe me. "Lil' buddy, your obsession with food will be the death of you and possibly me."

Chapter Twenty-Four

Christmas at Myrtlewood was spent with the same crowd of family and friends we'd had for Thanksgiving. Our motley crew was short one member however, as the elder Dr. Sawyer managed to end up in the hospital after a questionable encounter involving two old ladies at the senior center and a dozen long stemmed roses.

Junior had surprised us with a Christmas morning video call which meant, he assured us, his thirty-year attendance record was not broken. I had agreed, the streak was unbroken if only on a technicality, then fought back laughter as Mama commandeered my laptop for a nice long chat with Junior, her captive audience.

Madison had gone above and beyond during her forced hiatus at the plantation, and everything not decorated was spit shined and polished. She had a knack for decorating and exceptional organization skills.

Seeking respite from the boisterous pack, we'd wrapped ourselves in lap blankets and sought refuge in the gazebo that overlooked the river. I'd thanked her again for making Myrtlewood festive and teased her that the time spent in purgatory could lead to a new career.

"Funny you should mention a new career, Holly." Madison hunched her shoulders, bringing her fleece blanket closer to her ears as a strong gust carried chilly air off the water. "I have a meeting with my adviser when the new term starts."

"Oh? You aren't thinking of dropping out, are you?"

She shook her head. "No, but I am going to change my major. Instead of a criminal justice degree, I'm going to pursue prelaw."

My brows shot upward. "Going to be a lawyer instead of a cop?"

She nodded. "Yeah, being accused and almost charged with murder has left a bad taste in my mouth, especially where law enforcement is concerned."

"Madison." I sighed and gave her a one-armed hug. "Don't let this experience sour you. Being a peace officer is a rewarding career. Knowing you're helping your community to live safe, secure, and happy lives ... I wouldn't trade that experience for the world."

"I know, and I haven't ... I mean, I don't hate cops now or anything, it's just." She stared out at the water for a moment and, when she looked back at me, her eyes were blazing with a determined light. "I'm going to be an attorney, a *defense* attorney because no one should go through what I did!"

Her voice throbbed with emotion as she thumped her fist on the railing and stared out at the river. "We are a nation of laws, or we used to be. We believed in due process and the burden of proof. In this country, you are innocent until proven guilty by a jury of your peers." She glanced at me. "The media tried me in the court of public opinion! They told half-truths and twisted facts until people I've known all my life gave me a wide berth. I was stigmatized and verbally abused because it boosted their ratings. I'm going to fight against that by defending others and demanding that our Bill of Rights be respected."

My heart swelled with love and respect for Madison. She'd been through a horrible experience and came out stronger. She learned and grew and would now be a blessing to others who might find themselves in similar circumstances. Everything I'd done since finding Brianna Bellamy, from facing my fears with Roland to the hard feelings I'd caused in pursuit of justice, Madison's resolve was proof I'd done the right thing.

"An honorable goal, Maddie. Your father would be proud."

She sniffed and tucked her hair behind her ear as a particularly strong gust tried to blow us off our feet. "I hope so, Holly. His last months ... we didn't part on the best of terms, and I'll regret that for the rest of my life."

"Madison, your father loved you. What happened between y'all was entirely Brianna Bellamy's fault and she paid the ultimate price for her actions. Try and remember your father as he was before Brianna wormed her way into your lives and let the rest go." She nodded, and I could tell she'd accepted what I'd said, but I also knew it'd take time to let that advice take root.

Another blast of icy air swept over us, and I shivered. The timers kicked on, setting Myrtlewood's decorations aglow.

CAROLERS AND CORPSES

The plantation was full of friends, family, and holiday cheer—enough gloomy thoughts for one day. "Come on, kid, let's see if Dewey left us any chess pie!"

We'd returned to the warmth of the house and ended up playing a lively game of charades. The rest of the holiday weekend passed in a similar vein, but by a couple of days after Christmas, my extended family had set out for home, Mama and Dewey were back in Sanctuary Bay and The Colonel and I could relax and recoup before the whirlwind New Year's Eve events I had planned with Tate.

The days following the arrest of Kay Emory were hectic; the media even more frenzied. Luckily, Christmas was days away and we were able to retreat to Myrtlewood. But the peace was short lived as chaos of another kind arrived along with our guests.

With one part of the holiday finished, I could enjoy some time alone. The cold front that swept in for Christmas was long gone and we were back to balmy days and comfortable nights perfect for fireside reading.

The Colonel and I were taking advantage of just such a day by walking the property. He was frolicking among the saw palmetto and saplings while I stuck to the sandy track that ran from the front entrance to the boat dock and pondered the events that had consumed my holiday season.

The press had created a toxic environment that pitted neighbor against neighbor, and I prayed that, with Brianna Bellamy's killer arrested, things could get back to normal—or what passed for normal in Sanctuary Bay.

The weight of having the fate of Madison's future in my hands had been more pressure than I realized until it had lifted. I could breathe again and I resolved to never get involved in such a thing again!

My relationship with Junior seemed to be on the mend. His Christmas video call had gone a long way to satisfying Mama, and I lived my life by the motto that if Mama was happy, then everybody was happy. Mama's contentment aside, it felt like I had my son back and that was precious to me.

I could understand Kay Emory's actions, at least in so far as her grief over losing her son. Just being at odds with mine had taken a mental toll, but there my empathy ended.

Kay had allowed her own guilt and bitterness to consume her and lost her humanity in the process; I would be vigilant so that I didn't slide down that same path.

CAROLERS AND CORPSES

Guilt over driving the car that claimed her son's life was on par with what I imagined I should feel for having taken the life of Shawn Dupree. Yet, as I'd confessed to Roland as we shared a pizza at Mario's, I *didn't* feel guilty and, therefore, could not seek redemption.

My lack of shame bothered me because I didn't understand where it had gone, if in fact I'd ever felt it. Dr. Styles and even Connie seemed to think it stemmed from my having acted in self-defense but they weren't privy to my memories.

As I'd told Roland, I didn't remember shooting Shawn. And it was more than lack of memory, it was a gut feeling that I had not fired my weapon at all. That feeling, more than anything else, kept me awake at night.

Was it just a traumatized psyche as Dr. Styles insisted? Despite her insistence, I had tried to force the memories, but they never materialized during the waking hours. What haunted my dreams were twisted and disjointed vignettes that set my heart racing in terror.

The Colonel flushed a rabbit, drawing my attention to the present as he took off, leaving a trail of dust in his wake. He was relatively safe on our land; at least I had no fear of him being run over by a car or getting lost on an unfamiliar street.

However, there were miles of marsh surrounding Myrtlewood and dangerous critters living in the wetlands. I also had no desire to fish him out of the pluff mud nor spend hours washing the stink off his coat.

"Colonel! Heel!" I snorted, there was little chance my stubborn bulldog was going to be diverted by anything other than a pile of kibble or a bag of treats, so I gritted my teeth and forced my leg to accept a light trot as I trailed after him.

I'd reached the edge of the lawn when I spotted The Colonel on the front porch, tongue dragging and sides heaving. I was scolding him for leading me a merry chase when the crunch of gravel alerted me to a visitor.

I filled a water bowl for my errant dog, then plopped into a rocking chair and waited to see who had come calling. A white convertible came into view, crawling at a snail's pace down the sand covered drive.

My confusion turned to surprise as Roland Dupree parked beside my Scout and mounted the steps. "Afternoon, Roland. What brings you out to the island?"

He waved. "Hey, Holly. Stopped by The Oaks and Ms. Effie said I'd find you here. Hope you don't mind the intrusion."

CAROLERS AND CORPSES

"Of course not, can I get you a glass of tea? Something a little stronger? Think we still have some planter's punch from Christmas Eve."

He grinned. "Wooee, no thank you. That devil's brew should come with a warning label! You tryin' to get me a DUI?"

I laughed. "I stopped Dewey at one bottle of rum, but no sense takin' chances. Did you have a nice holiday?"

"I did, thanks for asking. Spent a couple of days in Columbia with my brother and his kids, and now I'm headed to Miami for a week at my condo; my reward for not starting any fights with family!"

"That sounds nice."

"Hmm, hope to do some fishing if the weather holds." He glanced coffee table. "Holly, about the other night ... I'm sorry if I was out of line or made you uncomfortable. I know I can get a little intense over Shawn's death."

"Roland, we've all just witnessed what can happen when a parent loses a child. As behaviors go, yours is entirely understandable." I sighed. "I just wish I could be of more help. I, well, I don't know if I'm ready to follow you down a rabbit hole and accept that there is something nefarious surrounding what happened. But, if it's any consolation, I have been trying to remember what happened."

Roland's brows rose. "And have you been successful? Anything new come back to you?"

Staring at The Colonel, now laying in the sun, I considered his question. I hadn't told anyone what the nightmare had revealed, hadn't really confronted those images in the light of day. Partly because I feared bringing on a panic episode but mostly because it felt intensely personal.

The memory that raised so many questions and terror was the time I lay bleeding and helpless on the forest floor.

But, if anyone had a right to know, it was Roland. I drew a deep breath and glanced at him. "I think I mentioned a nightmare I've been having ever since we ran into each other at the Christmas tree lighting?"

Roland nodded. "Yes, you did, though you didn't elaborate beyond telling me the dream concerned your movements after you drove onto my property."

Biting my lip, I debated one last time and then gave myself a mental shake. I needed to talk about what I'd seen in my dream, and, for some reason, instinct said I shouldn't tell Dr. Styles.

"It starts there, but what bothers me is what happens when I pull up on the pickup truck."

His brow furrowed. "Why does that part bother you so much?"

"I'm not sure." Images from my dream started to pop into my head. I gripped the arms of the rocking chair as my heart rate increased. My mouth was dry, and every muscle wanted to clench, as if bracing for impact.

Any time my body started to react I ran away from the memories, closed them off, changed the subject, practiced the DBT therapy; anything to avoid the panic response. But I was tired of fleeing, tired of unanswered questions, tired of doubting myself and my instincts.

I glanced at Roland. "Uh, if you're willing to," I shrugged, unable to find the words. "I'd like to remember my dream. If I start to remember while awake, I usually fight the memories for fear I'll have a panic attack, you know?"

"I understand, Holly. A friend was in a car bombing while stationed overseas and suffers from PTSD. Don't feel you have to—"

"No, I want to do this. For you, and for me." I shrugged. "Just, if things look like they're going south um, throw some water on me or something. Don't fancy having the rescue squad disturbing the neighbors."

Roland smiled. "Understood. I'll stop you if it gets out of hand."

With that assurance, though what he could do if I succumbed to a full-blown panic attack was anyone's guess, I closed my eyes and let my mind drift.

It took a few minutes of concentrating on my breathing and fixing the last image I routinely flashed back to in my mind but soon I was again on that shadow filled dirt road in the middle of a maritime forest.

I started to narrate what I was seeing, though my voice was barely above a whisper. "A shot rings out and I steer the car in the direction I think it came from. The sun is down and it's that twilight hour before full darkness descends but the tree canopy is heavy, and I can't see much beyond shadowy blurs outside the beams of my car lights."

"There's a curve in the road and when I come out of it, I'm blinded by high beams. A pickup truck is blocking the way. I pull the visor down but it doesn't do much good so I keep my eyes focused to the side of the road but ... in my periphery I can see someone standing near the driver's side, something moves, and I think maybe it's a person, maybe more than one."

My hands began to shake. I laced them together and squeezed, willing my fear to subside so I could continue. After several controlled breaths I continued.

"There's something laying in the road ... I think it must be a deer, but it seems too big and the wrong shape."

"What was it, Holly? Why was the shape wrong?"

I blinked and met Roland's gaze as I processed his question. "Um, I don't know, it's just always felt that way." I shrugged. "I've never attempted to analyze the flashbacks, I'm sorry."

Roland shook his head. "No, I'm sorry for interrupting. If you feel up to it, please continue. I'll hold my questions."

"Okay, maybe it will become clearer. I've had flashes of what I'm telling you before, it bothers me still, but not as much as what happens later."

He patted my clenched hands. "Tell as much or as little as makes you comfortable."

Another deep breath, a slow exhale, and I closed my eyes. "It's fully dark now, the only light is coming from the two vehicles. I can't see anything beyond what they hit. I have a bad feeling.

I want to turn around, but I push through my fear and drive closer, stopping about twenty yards from the truck."

My heart rate increased; my pulse drummed in my ears. I was powerless to stop my muscles from tensing, my body was going in to fight-or-flight mode and I considered stopping the trip down the memory lane from hell, but I reminded myself that Roland was there and he'd promised to take care of me. I could do this. I needed to do it.

"I leave the car running, I'm alert because something is very wrong, only I don't know what the threat is ... something moves beside the truck, and I snap open the holster and remove my weapon."

I opened my eyes and looked at Roland. "I've pulled my gun three times in my career. I didn't do that on a whim which is why ..." I shrugged and Roland nodded.

"I understand what you're implying. You can't remember or maybe you never knew, but whatever you rolled up on felt threatening."

"Exactly. I've tried to figure out what the threat was but ..." I gave up trying to find words to describe what I'd felt and returned to what I experienced that fateful night.

CAROLERS AND CORPSES

"Weapon out, I open the car door, keeping it between me and the line of fire. My gaze darts between the truck, whatever is laying in front of it, and the shadows by the side of the road."

A lump rose in my throat as the memories came faster. I knew what happened next, I'd relived it hundreds of times. "The radio squawks, drawing my attention for a split second and when I look back ... oh, God what is ... a shot, another, my ears are ringing, my leg is on fire ... I fall back toward the seat ... my head hits the door jamb, and everything goes black."

A warm hand covered mine. I swallowed hard and opened my eyes, meeting Roland's concerned gaze. We stared at each other, not speaking, as I fought to control my breathing.

After a few minutes, and one last shuddering breath, I nodded. Okay, I could do this, I wasn't alone, it was in the past.

"After I lost consciousness, everything after that is what fills my nightmares."

Roland frowned. "Do you feel up to going on? I'll understand if you don't."

"No, I told you, I want to know. I'm tired of being haunted. Maybe, if I can face whatever it is, I can ... I don't know. Move on? At least get a full night's sleep."

"Then know I'm here for you and proceed when you're ready."

I squeezed his hand in silent thanks and faced the ghost that haunted me. "I'm cold ... so cold, I can't feel my leg, but my other leg and hips are sticky with blood. I can smell it, metallic and earthy ... I want to throw up. There's chatter on the police radio and the engine ticks and hisses. Something is poking into my lower back; I roll over and moan as every nerve ending catches fire."

"A wave of nausea rolls over me and I close my eyes, desperate not to heave. Laying still calms my stomach and I realize I've been shot ... I have to move, get to the radio ... girding myself for the task I open my eyes and ... and ... oh dear God!"

I jerked and opened my eyes. "Roland ..." Tears welled and flowed down my cheeks. My stomach rolled and I struggled to catch my breath.

"Holly!" Roland jumped up and hovered over me. "Look at me, Holly, look, focus on my eyes! Deep breath in, then out, come on Holly Daye, snap out of it!"

I wrapped my arms around myself as violent tremors racked my body. I was locked in my nightmare. All I could see was the body in front of me, its vacant stare searing into my soul as my own life force flowed into the dusty road.

From a distance, I could hear Roland calling my name and telling me to breathe. The eyes that haunted me were fading, every breath seemed to make the terror recede, though Roland's hard shake might have hurried the process.

Several minutes went by, I was shaking like a leaf, The Colonel had nestled himself between my knees, and Roland rubbed my back and murmured something meant to soothe.

I concentrated on The Colonel, forcing myself to sync my breaths in time with his as I stroked his fur and let his warmth seep into my body.

When I was able to form a coherent thought, I drew a deep breath and looked up at Roland. My voice barely above a whisper and choking on the words, I told him what I'd seen.

"What I saw laying in the road ... Roland, your son was already dead."

The End

If you enjoyed Carolers and Corpses, The gang from Sanctuary Bay and I would appreciate a review!

The Holly Daye Mystery Series

Prequel

(Visit www.rachellynneauthor.com for details on how you can receive a FREE ebook)

Hounds and Heists

Book 1

Masquerades and Murder

Book 3

Priests and Poison

Book 4

Plantations and Allegations

Book 5

CAROLERS AND CORPSES

Scarecrows and Scandals

The Cosmic Café Mystery Series
Book 1

Ring of Lies
Book 2

Broken Chords
A Christmas Novella

Holly Jolly Jabbed

Eager to read the next installment in *The Holly Daye Mystery Series*?
Join the Cozy Crew Club Newsletter and hear about new releases,
happenings in the Cozy Mystery World, tidbits about my life and the Lowcountry I call home, as well as contests and giveaway opportunities.

RACHEL LYNNE

You'll also receive a FREE E-book Prequel in The Cosmic Café Mystery Series when you join!

Join the Cozy Crew Club Newsletter

or

www.rachellynneauthor.com

Made in the USA
Columbia, SC
29 October 2024